LILITH

LILITH

Brad Shprintz

Contents

Blanche Shprintz
(My Grandmother)
Thank you for your unconditional love.
You were taken very early in my life, yet your impact
was incredible. Thank you for the train rides to
downtown, the box lunches we had and all the toy store
visits you gave me.
I have never stopped missing and loving you!

1

HANNA - 6/26/24

The fragrance in the air was typical of mornings Hanna had in her youth, that freshness reminded her about the aftermath of a thunderstorm yet smelling sweeter and more beautiful. She had known she was different even at the early age of three, special in ways that made grownups act strangely. In that regard she was very self aware of herself, the animals on the farm, her brother and sister plus mom, dad, and the adults.

Hanna Freeman was thin, with long legs and straight hair that stretched to her waist. Her big brown eyes with her well-defined chin gave her a unique appearance. Her beauty was, different then whatever would be popular for the current fashion. She had her own look and style, beautiful and independent.

There was something else incredibly special about her that few others had yet was not observable by just looking at her appearance. Her fingers were delicate yet quite strong, in that regard, stronger than most of her peers. At twenty-four years around the sun, now a woman with many looking to be her partner.

She loved her youth, the morning chores, feeding the chickens, pigs and their one goat. Then the horses would need attending too. There was so much land that lay bare, free of buildings or other homes. Now looking back, realizing the lack of people also made it wonderful. Her effect on those around her was not natural which became known to her at an early age.

When she was around certain people, even if she said or had done nothing, exceptional things would happen for that person. There was the time she was visiting a friend, and they were playing in the kitchen. At the same time the friend's mother was making a cake for an annual baking contest, which she had never won. Her cakes would rank somewhere in the top five, once she gained second place, yet first always eluded her.

Hanna had asked her what she was doing, as she had seen her mother make many cakes without being so stressed concerning the creation. The lady explained it was a big contest, and she had never won, still she tried each year, so the making of her cake had to be perfect.

Looking into her eyes, being precocious for her age, Hanna said the following.

"Forget all your measurements, just mix it together. The secret is your thoughts, you must believe it is the best and make it with love thoughts." With that she smiled and became young again and ran off playing with her friend.

The woman had tried everything for years unsuccessfully, on a whim she had taken Hanna's advice. She started over from scratch, improvising in her measurements with all her feelings and thoughts on how everyone would love it. Her thoughts only about love for her cake and the judges who would be rating it.

After she had won, winning first place, she tried again the next year. Like usual she came in third. As the cake-lady review everything in her mind, she concluded that it must had been Hanna. A few years later Hanna could hear her mother having an argument with the cake-lady.

"No Hanna is busy; she has school assignments and other duties...I know it is important to you, but so are her studies. No, she is busy the entire week...I must go, goodbye."

That was an early example of what was to follow in dealing with people. If Hanna wished them success or just being near them, positive fortune followed. Regardless of the field they were working in, like magic they would have a break thru. Unfortunately for Hanna she gained nothing from it, sure she received their adulation and love yet nothing special happen for her.

Now she was on her own, which she really enjoyed. Of course, thoughts from her past, specially, when the days looked like this, beautiful with sweet fragrances from nature's garden.

Hanna did have an affinity to music, with the piano being her chosen instrument. She was such a natural she became a piano teacher, which provided good money and plenty of personal time.

She had just moved on from her last relationship and for the first time had met someone that she wanted to be around more than the reverse, which was the usual situation.

She thought about the man and woman, the one she wanted, and the one left behind. They were so different and yet she liked them both. Then from out of nowhere she had a thought about the old man who always stared at her, when she went shopping for groceries. It made her feel uncomfortable, she never looked at him, while moving quickly past him to enter the store.

The old man parked in the front, just sitting on his motorcycle, smoking, and watching the people pass by. A few times she was free of his eyes, yet it was uncanny how often she would see him as he would gaze at her.

Hanna last relationship was with a woman artist. She painted not in shapes but colors. The real beauty was the mixture of colors and textures combined with the heavy paints that she used. When Hanna met her, she was close but never created anything remarkable.

Watching her paint was amazing. Most abstracts paintings look like the artist was very free of hand while creating it. Hanna's girlfriend was just the opposite. She thought about each color and stroke before carefully applying it to the canvas.

To Hanna, once they benefited from being around her, then the problems would begin. It would show itself differently depending on the person, yet the results regardless of how it revealed itself, were always negative. Those effects usually started slowly yet would grow in intensity and frequency.

One day Hanna came up behind her girlfriend while she was painting. At first, she did not want to be distracted by Hanna's attention. She gave her a kiss on the neck and then pulled out a blindfold. Now the artist objected but after some sweet words and kisses, she agreed.

Then Hanna told her, "You know where your paints are, now paint with your mind, forget and remember at the same time." With that she guided her hand holding the brush.

"Now just go with your instincts, paint with your heart." Hanna was now giving her a mini back rub while the artist became more into the feeling of painting with brush stokes in her head while her eyes saw nothing. Her excitement of this new feeling gave her paints passion they had never felt. Also, her body being touched while she painted filled her mind with pleasure.

The result was incredible, you could see and feel the pleasure in the painting. If could not be replicated, as its birth was a gestalt of many different elements, one of them being love. It was a masterpiece, the best work the artist ever created.

Once shown to the public there became a bidding war at the art gallery, a star had been born. Unfortunately, this would be a shooting star, for without Hanna's delicate touch and presence near the artist, the process would not work.

That is when the negative side would start to show itself. Like the cake-lady from the past, the artist now always wanted Hanna's help, her touch, her power to keep recreating those special moments.

It became clear that whatever started as love or affection turned into greed for fame and fortune. Now transformed into an ugly view of its former beauty. Caring for Hanna morphed into a desperate need for more attention to the artist own work.

This experience happened often making Hanna only want to surround herself with the friends she grew up with, the animals on the farm, dogs, cats, and birds. Most creatures except humans were her chosen desire. That was until she met him.

KNIGHT IN SHINNING ARMOR

Adam Knight was different than anyone else she had ever met. She had never felt instant love as she felt for him. Everything about him was special, even his name. Adam which reminded her of the first man in the Garden of Eden, it was a noble strong name. Knight being heroic, a person doing good for others. To her she could not imagine a better name for his title.

He was perfect, until then only her father had that status. She closed her eyes to relive how they had met.

There was a line of stores, the usual ones that group together, a bank, a woman's hair salon plus a pizza restaurant and others along those lines. Hanna had park far from her destination as she liked parking spots less crowded and enjoyed walking. Usually, she had a swift pace having her focus on her target with no distractions.

That day was different, like someone inside her head, saying slow down, there is more to see than just where you are going. She then noticed how beautiful the day was, with weather that would be the envy of anyone anywhere.

Off the center store appeared three bikers from a motorcycle club plus four police officers, with one of the bikers already handcuffed and directed into the back of a police car. At that point, the biker's friends were very agitated while the officers were sorting through the affair.

Even Hanna who was still thirty-five feet away, could feel the tension in the air. Like more trouble was coming and it would only be moments before the new action would occur.

That is when Adam coming from the pizzeria involved himself in the tense situation around him. Most would have avoided that scene, but he went right to the bikers not yet in handcuffs.

The first thought Hanna had was, at this point she did not know his name, *that man approaching the bikers was not noticeably big or strong. Yet his stride was wide, showing no fear in his encounter with them.* After a brief conversation he then with the same type of strut, marched over to the police.

Hanna was thinking, *now that is always a dangerous move, you can never know which way that will go, the best is you walk away, and the worst is your in the back seat with no way out.*

That was one of the aspects that grab her attention about him. He was fearless, he had an extended conversation with one of the officers. After a bit of time, he pulled out his phone and then things changed. The biker prisoner in the back seat of the patrol car, was released from both the car and handcuffs.

As soon as the biker was back with his friends they left quickly. The police left extremely fast also, and one minute later, it was like it never happened.

Hanna was feeling something she rarely felt, and with an impulsive act, she rushed over to Adam. She had never thought of getting someone number or trying to get a date with anyone. Most people just wanted to be around her. And after a brief time, as their life improved, never wanted her out of their sight.

She had never been impulsive, having a colder approach to new things and ways. It felt like the entire world was watching her, judging to see if she had what it takes to make the moment.

Now she was making things up as she went ahead, in an area she had never ventured into before.

"Hey," and then after a few seconds, "How about dinner, I'll pay." That ended with a smile, which Hanna did not do or give often.

Adam taken in by her smile, he was initially on his guard, for doing spy work for the government you never know when someone is trying to compromise you. To Adam this was more intense than preventing the earlier trouble.

Truth, it is hard for anyone to not be receptive to someone who is extremely attractive while at the same time, wanting your attention. Hanna's smile was beautiful, it had a mixture of innocence and letting one's guard down.

Adam thought to himself, *how many men have been destroyed for want of that smile*, then with his own smile in return.

"Sure, but I will pay for us both!"

Hanna had frozen for a couple of seconds, like she had heard him but was still processing the information much slower than normal.

"What time would you like to go, do you want to pick me up?"

Adam replied, "Yes to the second question, what time is good for you?"

With that they exchange numbers with each going on their separate ways. They may have been traveling in different directions physically but mentally they were in each other's minds.

Hanna had never been in love, not the type of love she was now feeling. Her mind tried to make sense of all the emotions flooding and overwhelming her being. How could just meeting someone elicit so much joy? She had watched love stories on television and at the movies. Not being a fan of reading, those other avenues she explored.

It did not seem real to her, like the actors were always just pretending to be head over heels in love with someone they barely knew. Now she was the actor, and it was real. Thinking about what to wear, how to do her hair, and so many other details, that now were major priorities.

And yet it was wonderful, better than anything she could explain. She thought, *it is like the best thing you can imagine and than 100 times better than that.*

Love makes everything prettier, easier to deal with the day-to-day troubles we all encounter. There truly is a glow about people in love, easy to see even in strangers. Hanna had that glow, now traveling on a road with heart.

Her phone rang with her artist friend, wanting her to come over, saying she had fixed something special, something she really would love. That is the way it had become, imploring her to come, promising any and everything to make it happen.

Hanna's thoughts were on what she would wear, as she usually wore jeans, yet she had skirts and dresses used for more special or relaxed occasions. Before getting serious about her attire, her old love, x-love, would have to be handled.

That was not unusual for her, as everyone she became close to, ending up becoming obsessed with keeping their relationship going. She had a mode she went into, firm and unwavering, she had found that attitude was the only way. And at times even that did not work.

"Honey, we have talked about this, you need to move on." Hanna was polite with directness being her guide. She like to get to the point where others would be less straightforward.

Now the pleading began, she waited, hoping after the rant it would help her with accepting what now will never be, their time together was over.

In some ways Hanna never really felt what her left behinds experienced. No one had ever wanted to leave her once a relationship was established. She was introspective and thought, *can one really know what someone else feels. Yes, the outside can show tears or such types of sadness. Yet the real thoughts in the mind and heart from a partner can only be experience in singular form.*

After much internal debate she decided on a cream color tight fitting summer dress. It ended three inches above her knees and looked wonderful on her. Hanna's type of built being thin everywhere except her buttocks, which in its own way was perfect.

She never wore makeup but on special occasions she did apply it sparingly, this being that type of occasion. It was a new experience being so excited to meet a stranger. There was no fear just adrenaline for its beginning.

She thought, *her Adam Knight would never hurt her, he was a prince, a noble warrior doing charitable deeds.* Smiling and laughing at herself for becoming so swept away by her new and in her mind, only love.

Life can be so different when in love, beautiful things come alive, whether it is the landscape or a stranger's kindness. The mind giving the body extra energy, having a feeling that nothing is impossible.

Hanna was ready now just waiting for that phone call that will change her life forever. Waiting also changes when in love, each moment becoming more intense than the last. Hearing, seeing, just knowing that your true love is good, in that regard, everything becomes special.

THE OLD MAN - 3/12/2024

All cities have their areas, places that are outside of the law or at least will take a major operation to enter and police it. Good people do not go there, and bad people can fend for themselves, leaving it devoid of a local authority's presence.

The gang that owned that neighborhood were hanging out on what they called the wall. Being a small group and claiming an area that no one else wanted or cared about. When you have nothing, anything becomes something, which then becomes worth defending.

Their wall being just a stone structure in front of one of the largest old homes there. Drinking and smoking was their work at that moment.

Everything was normal until it was not, life has a way of changing from real to quasi real in a blink.

Nobody saw him approach, nothing and then he was there. Laying in front of the house across from them, on the lawn halfway between the home's door and the walkway following the street.

He slowly stood up, slightly bent, obviously old yet there was also something else. It could not be put into words, there was a presence about him. He was looking over himself, like he was doing an inspection as if he had lost something.

Of course, to the men on the wall this incursion would not be acceptable. Five men rose and walked over and surrounded him, before their fun would begin.

Right before violence will occur, it had its own feeling, like electricity waiting to explode. Now that time had arrived as their second in command began.

"You think you can just come here like you own it? This is ours!"

The old man, who had not taken his eyes off the man in front speaking to him, replied.

"I am leaving."

Now the young man made a big show of his words, "Boys you hear, he is leaving!" Then after a long moment, with his face changing from a smirking smile to evil intentions.

"Oh, you're leaving, and we are going to be nice enough to give you a lesson in respect!"

With that the speaker acted like he was turning away only to telegraph a wide hard right-hand squeezed into a fist aimed at the old man's face.

At first the old man did not move, yet his movements were subtle, with his right foot came a short unstoppable kick, for the distance was so close that no movement by the intended victim could restrain it from its target the kneecap. While this was happening at the same time his body slightly moved to the left while his right arm pushed and then pulled the attacker's arm. Together with the kneecap hit plus the weight of the intended sucker punch missing and then directed straight to the ground.

He hit hard, headfirst, and not realizing yet that his leg, would now no longer function. For a split moment everyone was frozen, taking in what just happened so quickly. Here not only did their companion not strike the blow but now looked like he was in serious trouble.

The old man hardly moved and looked just as he had before the ruckus. Obviously, he had been in much violence in his past. Then as if there was an unheard message given to everyone left standing, they started to attack him from all sides. He went down quickly, and the punishment began. It lasted for about five minutes, if watched it would have seemed much longer. So many kicks to the body and head. Then the baseball bats, which brought over from the few left that were still sitting on the wall, began.

The old man acted like a turtle, with the sole purpose of covering up. Trying to protect his head with his arms and his organs by giving them his back to hit. Even the gang started to get tired of the beat down and then looked to their leader, to see what should happen next.

One of the thugs pulled out his gun, pointed it to the old man's head, not more than five inches while asking, "You want him dead?"

Before an answer given, sirens started sounding, they came from different directions, all getting louder towards one spot. Their wall was the recipient of that noise.

The leader was not afraid of the police, he was thinking that killing someone should have some value to it. The old man had nothing which factor into his decision. He moved his head from left to right, signaling a bit more life for the old man.

When the police arrived, they were all sitting on their wall. There were three police cars with five officers.

Three officers went over to the gang while two went to the man laying flat on the lawn across the street.

"What happened here? Asked the officer.

"Just some old drunk fool that fell down."

Wondering why he asked, knowing he would get nothing pertinent from them and assuming they were the cause of it, he went over to the pair inspecting the victim.

"Is he dead? I wonder who called this in? Asked the man who had just spoken with the suspected suspects.

"No, he is alive, barely." Answered one of the men who had gone straight to inspect the victim.

"Let's just take him to the hospital and dump him at the ER. I don't mind if you put him in my car and I will do the rest."

"Sure, but we could just call for EMS and let them handle it."

"Frankly, I do not want to hang around, hate this area and I am hungry. It will take less time to drop him off then to wait for the EMS. Then I am going to eat."

They moved him into the back seat and the old man was dropped off at the ER as a John Doe. He had no information on him of any kind, no watch, phone, or wallet, figuring the hospital would do the prints and sort it all out.

2

THE DINNER - 6/26/24

Adam Knight's mind went to his first and only love, who now was gone, Jayne Stillwater. She had died and, in that death, killed all his dreams of a wonderful life with his true love.

His thoughts went to how some people can make such a dramatic difference in other's lives. He had met a person like that, and with that connection his whole life changed. Jayne was part of that change. Never had he fallen madly in love, only in the end to be abandoned and left to fair for himself, alone. *Jayne had left for the Final Battle, and although it was won, her life was lost,* those thoughts lived in his mind daily.

Thinking to himself, *can anyone truly get over their first love?*

He used to be a very average person, holding a job down while trying to find some pleasures in life. His new occupation, now his passion had changed his thinking about life. To live without passion now felt worthless. And then there were the excitement of his missions. Never knowing when things might go bad and responding appropriately.

He thoughts continued, *there is so much to know and learn about spying.* One of the down sides was the added paranoia that comes with the job. In his mind, *there being only two groups, spies like himself with alternatively motives and civilians.*

The civilians were everyone else, police, politicians, lawyers, teachers etc. Anyone not in the spy game. So, the first order of business, is to decide which group the people he is dealing with belonged to.

Now his thoughts went to Hanna, who he had just finished calling. There had been others before her who tried to get his attention. That also was a change from his former life, it appeared others could tell he was not ordinary.

Hanna Freeman was different, his clairvoyant abilities told him she would make an enormous difference in his future. Besides that, he felt a special energy around her, and then there was her beauty. Like all her other features, special in its own way.

It was obvious she wanted to be with him, which at first raised some red flags. Then like most people, men especially, his mind convinced him that all his great traits lured people to him. Even with that Adam was smart enough not to let his fantasy thoughts overwhelm his good judgment.

He was slim with five feet ten inches for height, and having brown hair that in the light had a reddish look, that with a mustache and beard gave him an Irish appearance.

Hanna was agreeable to whatever he wanted; he did try to find out what food she liked but she only wanted him to be happy. It is extremely hard not to like someone who appears to care about your happiness as their first concern.

Being honest to himself he thought, that always was an issue with Jayne, her being committed more to her causes then to his concerns. It was very enjoyable to find someone like Hanna, then reminded himself, she found him.

Living in District of Columbia has many restaurants of all kinds, making it appear that every nationality had representation. He decided to go to his favorite Italian restaurant; they made a fabulous Veal Francis.

All their Veal dishes were excellent, and Adam had eaten there often, developing a friendship with one of the owners. That was one of Adam's talents, he had a very easy-going attitude, making fast relationships.

The owner related that the secret was in the pans. They had been using the same pans for decades, which had built up something that just made the Veal dishes incredible. He said that they were never put into the dishwasher and carefully cleaned by hand.

Adam never had gone on many dates before his life changed, and after that still rarely did. His line of work was always exciting even with the boring parts, yet this was different. It was not the fear of death or failure but just true excitement of what the night and future may bring.

He drove over to her place, parked, and walked to her door. He had only seen her once before that day and it was brief. When Hanna appeared in the entrance to her apartment, he realized his memory had failed him. She looked like the most beautiful woman he had ever seen. His breath and voice were gone with only his smile staying.

Hanna invited him inside her home and instantly rush to his chest, giving him a sweet hug.

There is a feeling that the body knows, much better than the mind. When someone gives you a hug and it is exactly right, how both bodies fit together perfectly. Being close to that person means more than anything. And the right amount of pressure in the squeeze, all these aspects plus more, are known by the body.

Hanna felt right in his arms, she was surprisingly strong while also being sweet and tender. As she released him, for Adam had no intentions of letting go, she gave him a brief kiss on his cheek, near his ear.

Once they arrived at the Italian restaurant, which was really a private club having very exclusive patrons. Its atmosphere suited the love that Hanna had for Adam. Amour was in the air, Adam now had no thoughts of his past love, Jayne. Hanna was everything Jayne was not, making him the main attraction, feeling like a superhero.

First thing she wanted to know was what did he do to resolve the problem between the police officers and the bikers. Also adding it was extremely brave of him to get involved at all.

"Most would have walked away, you not only went there, but you also help the bikers! What did you say?"

Hanna did have a rebel streak, with authority not welcomed. On the farm there never was a need for law enforcement. The only time they were seen was to inform them of some new restrictions.

Neither had their phones out with their eyes solely on each other.

Hanna sat there waiting for his answer, her complete focus on his face and what he would say. She was raised the old-fashioned way and listening meant really doing that. Full attention on the speaker.

Adam with a big smile and trying to be humble began.

"Well, I did not do very much, I asked the bikers what happened. Hearing that their friend had given the police officers the finger and then had been cuffed. I felt I should help him. I told them to leave quickly once their friend is back if that would be okay, and they agreed."

Adam had paused and then resumed; Hanna was giving him a look that he was wonderful.

"So, I asked the police who was in charge and tried to make him understand the law." Then Adam started laughing and continued.

"After that failed, I went the other route. I know many people in this town. I told him to stop me when I mention a name he is aware of. After the third name he recognized the fourth and the fifth was his boss. They fourth his boss's boss and the third that boss's boss. I opened my phone and said I was going to call the third name and let it all rain downhill. Or he could release the biker, and all was good. The police officer decided quickly, it was better to release the biker and that was that."

What Adam did not tell her was he had clairvoyant abilities and had a premonition that gunfire was coming if that situation had not been amicably settled.

Hanna was amazed at how smart and resourceful her Adam was. In that moment she had decided he would forever be in her life. His caring for others with no concern for his own safety was so rare in this modern age.

Adam tried his best to get Hanna talking about herself or anything else. She was so genuinely interested in all aspects of his life. Making it quite easy to expound on many different subjects that were on his mind.

She talked about her tattoos and how it really was not that painful to get, and her love for animals of all types also came out. It was a conscious plan on her part, for as Adam was driving her home, he realized that she was very mysterious.

It is a mistake to reveal so much about oneself via social media or just verbalizing everything going on in your world. Having mystery not only makes others more interested in you but also allows you to not be tied down to any known group. It is the gift of freedom. Those thoughts were in Adam's mind, now doing spy work, half the art is never revealing too much.

So many new questions came into his mind about Hanna. He thought *being a piano teacher is a great cover for a spy if you can play the piano!*

When he arrived at her home, Hanna insisted he stop in before he left for the night.

Her apartment had many candles, first she made him sit on the couch, while she lit them all. Then Hanna changed the lights from a soft white to multiple colors which slowly jumped from one bulb to another. Lastly, she put some music on and returned to Adam on the couch.

Between the way the candles changed colors while the walls also had a flickering turned it into a magic moment. Hanna looked at him, waiting for her kiss. She believed that her chosen one, which she hoped, and thought Adam was, would give her a kiss that would be the best kiss anyone could ever receive.

Her last partner was a great kisser, so Hanna had experienced that, she could not put it into thoughts what she hoped would happen. Just that it would be something she had never experienced before.

Adam started to lean in towards her body their faces getting closer, Hanna had closed her eyes letting everything happen without her control.

Their first kiss did not disappoint either, both were good at that, which is for most a unique talent that is not taught. In Adam's mind, it was amazing, he had never been kissed as Hanna had kissed him. His thoughts went to incredible, fantastic; words of that nature flooded his mind as his body was loving the experience.

To Hanna, it was so much more than the physical pleasure. In her mind all things are composed of the physical and mental aspects, which then combined to produce a final result. The significant difference between him and her girlfriend was the mental part.

Yes, the physical part was great yet there was more, her mind also had pleasure like she had never felt. Serenity and love combined that was much more than just a kiss.

When Adam left both were different then just hours before. Their minds were racing with thoughts of each other.

JOHN DOE 3/12/2024

The hospital was big, also connected to a university, having plenty of money and remarkable talent. The old man was dropped off at the ER, now he was their concern, thought the police officer as he went to his lunch.

Since he was unable or unwilling to talk, beat up and near death, they ran a complete head and body scan to figure out what injuries he might have. Amazingly there were no internal organ damage, yes, his face and body looked horrible. And he was in great pain yet that would all heal.

The incredible feature was inside his head. That being an exceptionally large chip connected to his brain. Not like the chips you would see in a computer, whatever it was, it was not natural. They had a top neurologist connected to both the hospital and university that they contacted about the issue.

The neurologist checked the x-rays, then had him moved to the newest wing of the hospital. That section having the latest technologies, which included electronic door locks, cameras inside the room, plus outside showing the hallway and room door.

It was a little pass 3 o'clock in the morning, he was going to contact his college friend who had done quite well for himself in the government. He wanted to impress him, to show him that being a neurologist had its share of the unknown and unusual. Figuring it would be more proper to wait until 6 or 7 and wanting to do more research on the patient before he contacted him.

The neurologist had the patient's door locked electronically and then investigated his fingerprint results. That also came back with a surprise. Connected to the name was a special note to contact the Senior Advisor to the President with a number to call ASAP.

Knowing he was going to call in 3 hours, and that the patient's door was locked, plus with the security of the cameras. He thought what harm can a few hours make. He was the kind of man that figured he knew everything, that his judgment or any opinions he had, were right and the only opinions to have. He would not panic and call as soon as he read that on the fingerprint id report. It seemed no one else had read or called it either.

At six in the morning, he contacted the number on the report and was surprised who responded. It was his college friend; he knew he had a prominent position in the government but never really knew his title.

His phone call answered with, "Hello, James Bucket how can I help you?"

After the neurologist identified himself, mentioning what a small world it was, he related the information about the patient accepted as John Doe.

"So, you see, I was going to contact you anyhow about the unusual technology within his head."

James being serious, which was also his normal state in college, replied with the following.

"Put a guard outside his door, I am sending a team to transfer him to our facility. When did you find out this information?"

"About 3 am, his door is locked, and we have a video feed of the door and hallway from the outside. He can barely walk, there is no reason to be concerned and your welcome."

James just replied, "You should have called at 3. We also want all his information, including any tests you have performed, thank you."

The neurologist was upset that James would question his judgment, just to make sure everything proceeded without problems, he personally went to the patient's room. He was not prepared for all the surprises that followed.

First, twelve soldiers dressed in all black came marching to the door of patient John Doe. They had all types of weapons and looked like they were prepared for a war to erupt.

Their leader demanded that the door be unlocked so they could transport John Doe.

When the door opened, the room was empty. The neurologist could not believe it, searching the room and closet, then angrily contacted the hospital security force, demanding to understand how this could happen.

While that was happening the leader of the soldiers were in communication with James conveying the current situation and what he wanted done next.

It was initially determined that it must have been an inside job and that their electronic surveillance had been compromised. The door unlocked electronically, and the live feeds were playing a loop from the past while not showing the present.

James was already checking outside surveillance to pick up the trail after he left the hospital. Later it was seen that he walked out the front door in his street clothes with the help of a walker. Once outside he disappeared into the darkness. The last point of observation was forwarded to a different team then the soldiers, hoping they could pick up his trial.

CLARA 3/13/2024

Being in her mid-fifties, Clara had experienced much in her life. As a child she would collect chestnuts just so she could give them to the squirrels in the fall. There were the great moments and her long-lasting marriage, yet it was not without hardships. Unlike so many that can become bitter about life's treatment, especially when it brings burdens that most do not have to bear.

Clara was special, she was a bright color on a dark painting. She had a love for fixing things, especially people in need. Where most would be afraid of appearances, the ugly and scary ones, that only brought her compassion out more.

Later she would say it was fate, something that would happen only once for many varied reasons. There was a detour, and it was late at night or early in the morning, depending on your perspective. She usually would not be driving at that time, but her friend needed help. Her relationship with her husband was strong. They had love for each other, even after 35 years, a trust in each other that real relationships always have.

Not only did her tire go flat, but it also happened at the darkest part of the road. She thought about calling her husband, yet she hated to bother him. She was not worried about getting dirty, just it was so dark which gave the surroundings a scary feeling. Also, when areas are deserted, trouble feels like it has a free pass to do whatever it wishes.

She got out of her car walking to the passenger's rear tire, inspected the flat herself and was about to make a call when the most unexpected thing happened.

It was a black night, where the darkness ate the small light that was brave enough to show itself. She had pulled out her phone with its screen acting like a torch in that darkness.

"Please help!" It was a man's voice, an old man who was in pain, yet she could see no one.

"Where are you? What do you need help with?" Clara had a voice that match her personality, it was nice, not squeaky, or heavy.

"In the bushes, need place to recover, beat up by a gang."

She could tell there was pain in each word, she wanted to help but was intimidated. The whole scene reminded her of Abraham and the burning bush. She was talking to a bush without seeing the person.

"We are close to a hospital; I can take you there." She said it with love in her voice, like a mother who has found a lost child and is trying to get that child to safety.

"No!" It was said louder than all his earlier spoken words. Said with such forcefulness that it obviously brought physical pain to his being.

"Let me see you, I can drop you off at a motel." For someone she did not know, and had no commitment or loyalty to, Clara really was trying to help him.

"My face is scary looking, do you have a shed or garage, even just a secluded area in the back of your home?" All this was said in pain, as if each word was a challenge to utter.

At this point, Clara had lost her fear of him attacking her. From the sound of his voice, he was fighting just to stay alive.

"Well, I will help you out, but I still have to change this tire, before we can go." She later could not explain why she agreed to help him. She described it like a voice in her head, that would hear her fears and then answer them with reassurances that those concerns would not occur. It was impulsive yet to her felt thought out.

Even with her strong marriage and her husband being aware of her wanting to help others, it was an awkward conversation she had with him when she returned home.

She changed the flat, with extra energy derived from the man in the bushes. She wanted to see his face, yet he would only come out when the car was ready to go. Trying to act brave she was now ready to resume her journey, just waiting for him to leave his hideout.

His face was awful, busted lips, bruised eyes, one not able to open because of the swelling. His nose and ears were damaged, and any other part not mentioned still looked bad. After a few seconds of shock, she told herself as trying to reassure her decisions, *it is what the inside looks like, not the outside.* She really could not explain why she wanted to help this old beat-up man. At her age, she did more things in her life now that just felt right, everything did not have to add up.

She helped him to her car, he insisted on laying down on the floor, in the back seat which she assumed was to hide him better during the drive. For a moment she became scared again, it was an irrational fear, he was in bad shape and could hurt no one.

Little was spoken during the ride home; she parked inside the garage and asked him to wait there while she talked to her husband.

"Thank you, the garage is fine." As he said that he found a corner that had a couch. That part of the garage was her husband's man cave. Once the old man was on the couch, he instantly fell asleep. She grabbed a blanket from one of the shelves, laid it over him, and went to talk with her husband.

3

NICHOLAS BOLT 3/13/ 2024

Nicholas was his formal name, he preferred Nick, everyone just called him Mr. Bolt or sir. He always wanted power, which given to a good man is not a terrible thing. Never dreaming that one day he would be chosen to fill the coveted spot of Senior Advisor to the President.

Bolt was not connected to any president; he was the real power of the government. To him the president was just a distraction, so the real work will not be detected. He was the head of the black ops, plus so much more.

Now that he thought about it, his predecessor Sam Smith, never actually talked about the president, to the point making it feel like that position did not matter. Bolt was not formally introduced to any members of the government. But there was a difference, he knew what they were doing, while they never knew or dare question what he had done.

There was no question he was above them, in charge. Bolt Achilles's heel was his love, or lust for power. It can corrupt even good hearts.

James Bucket worked under Bolt, he was top in his class, a no nonsense very focus person. James understood how vital the work he was involved in mattered. How serious negative outcomes can be devastating to many. He was always serious but never more so than now, working for Nicholas Bolt.

He was giving Bolt a debriefing on what just happened. Thinking to himself, that he had never seen Bolt so concerned, so troubled about something that had not cause any problems. Then again, he had read all the information about the old man, realizing they had an exceptionally long relationship between the two, as Bolt was his handler.

Also, his file was unreal, with parts even blocked out to James's lack of high enough security clearance. What he was able to read was astonishing, with now having so many unanswered questions.

"Sir it is only a matter of time before he will be located, do you want him apprehended or just observed?" It was a logical question, brought down to the extreme basic, to do something or nothing.

"Constant observation with no interactions!" *This man affected Bolt*; those were the thoughts of James. Then just to confirm his observation, Bolt declared firmly.

"Dismissed." Which again was not like their usual interactions. It reminded James of when someone gets rattled and loses their usual persona.

James's thoughts went to their more pressing problem, *Lilith*. He was hoping they would have discussed different strategies in dealing or coping with her.

JAYNE STILLWATER 5/1/2024

There are people that inspire others not just with what they have done, but with why they chose to do it in the first place. To say Jayne was special would be an understatement. She was an inspiration to all who knew her.

Jayne's feelings about love were in a cause, a purpose bigger than just reaching one's personal gratification. It had to be something that others would gain from equally or more than the person providing it.

In the past and still now, people who joined the Peace Corps or missionaries to go to areas in need of help, whether it is building structures, teaching, and medical services, or spiritual enlightenment. Where most in society have the attitude of why would I do that, what is in it for me?

People like Jayne, saw others' happiness as the greatest form of love that can be achieved.

Jayne's story built upon the crossroads of contradictions and un-believable. Her age was in the mid forties, yet she looked no older than thirty-three. Partly due to her genetics but also to the fact that most of her life she had lived in space, upon a ship called the Nevermore. Moving at great speeds while dealing with less gravity forces than upon Earth, gave her a younger appearance.

She trained from her earliest days as a soldier, a person within a group that had a higher purpose then just trying to collect money or things like love. Their missions had meaning, they would help others with sometimes being the difference in saving their lives.

After her last adventure, which was on a planet called Fattalla, they had now brought her back to Earth, which never felt like her home. During her last mission she had met a man named Adam. Her mind thought about him often, yet knowing if he knew she was alive, it would all start again.

His type of love and her feelings about love just never could truly flourish. Then thinking to herself, *flourish, it was smothering*. She knew he was jealous of everyone around her, even old men, which made her smile.

If Adam had known her better, old men were not her type. *Certain old men do demand respect for their position or accomplishments* were her thoughts. Like her CW, her old captain of the Nevermore. It was not love but such strong admiration for that man, that others might con-fused her feelings.

All people have thoughts of what if, having so many different paths, generating too many outcomes to contemplate. Her training as a soldier was to accept most things, except for imprisonment, while still getting your primary agenda completed.

A thought entered her head, making her smile and laugh at herself. It was a picture of a curb-way with a drainage system about a foot from the curb, being in the street, using a metal plate plus an opening directly across in the curb-way to remove the water.

There was a stream of water running against the curb in the street until about 3 inches before it would have entered the drainage plate. Then it made a 90 degree turn to the left until it was about 2 inches past the metal plate. Again, another turn to the right, running parallel to the drainage plate, it went straight that way until the plate ended and then made a hard right, reached the curb, and continued straight down the street.

It was like it knew about the plate's function to remove it, while the water still avoided it, with no problem at all. Between the architects, builders, and planners, all of that had no effect on collecting water that did not want to be removed.

She felt like that water, going her own way, regardless of what others had put in place to stop her. Thinking to herself, *in life we do not see the drainage plate yet like the water avoiding it, we move efficiently around it.*

She would always have affection for Adam, yet her life and desires would push her where she needed to go, just like the water that refused to be collected and removed.

Currently she was working for another old man, which made her giggle to herself, thinking, *why am I always around or working for old men.* In this case, the old man had an immensely powerful position and was extremely nice to her.

She remembered Bolt saying to her, "Just tell me what you want to do, and where. There is only one restriction, which we both want." He waited patiently for Jayne, who was not expecting to call her own future.

She had been a soldier plus held many other titles. After her time in the Final Battle, fighting next to her CW, while seeing so many killed in battle, including her hero, that life was over. Jayne liked using her hands, so it became a choice of building or farming, with building winning.

She chose Australia, which is a unique place upon Earth. Apparently Bolt had connections everywhere and knew somebody for her to contact once she arrived there.

Jayne had seen more death than most soldiers, even ones that spent all their time on the front lines. She thought about how most who never been there, glorified war, acting like it was a movie and once view, on to the next thing.

It is after the battles, once your back home, that the real pain of loss begins. Trying to be normal and wash out those memories of the left-behinds. She was happy with her choice and enjoyed working construction. Feeling like she had really started a new life, her old one would never be forgotten, but living in the past eliminated the present or potential futures.

GETTING INFORMATION 6/28/2024

Adam was working on a mission locally. His boss, Nickolas Bolt, treated him well and seemed to take an active interest in his happiness. Adam's mind was not on his mission but on Hanna.

He did have access to big data, which is detailed information about everyone on the planet. But he did not want to access it, first there is always a trail when finding information on someone. If he went that route, it could become known to his boss or others.

Now that he was doing spy work, part of that process was thinking about how not to reveal information to most around him. On the other hand, trying to keep something private was extremely hard in today's world.

He decided to just do it as a civilian would. He used his browser in anonymous mode, going to her Facebook page. She did have one, which was a start, it had not been updated in many years. There were no pictures of her or entries. Just one picture of a goat facing the camera. It was a dead end, but she did have some friends connected to her account.

Now going into each friend's page to see if there were any cross references to Hanna. There he did have some success, finding three pictures of her on her friends' pages. He also learned that she excelled in math and was quite accomplished also playing the guitar. Another thing he learned was her birthday being less than a month away.

There was no question he was getting her a gift, but he wanted it to be something she really liked. The type of present that would show her he was worthy of her love.

They were meeting again tomorrow, going to a park to enjoy the scenery and each other company. Hoping he would find out more about her directly. Feeling like he was now living his best life, that is what love can do. Its power to change even good times into the greatest experience of living.

Now his mind went back to his current mission, he had already infiltrated his target's group. It had taken over five months, yet he now had worked into their inner core. Most groups or organizations have a small circle of people that control their essential information and actions that group will take in the future.

His mission being to destroy that group from the inside, which really is the easiest way in conquering an enemy. They were terrorists wanting to disrupt the country, breaking down the grid by using extraordinarily strong EMPs otherwise known as an electromagnetic pulse.

The terrorist target was the power grid, figuring that if the power goes out long enough, 3 to 5 weeks, the citizens will start killing each other, just for food. Without electricity so many resources would collapse. That being the beauty of it, like a single match that lights the forest into a blaze.

All that was forgotten as he visualized his future date with Hanna. Time now moving quickly as he was in deep thought. There are times when in contemplation that time changes its speed. This being that time as now it was late in the evening, Adam thinking that he had drifted off into sleep, and then reemerged without realizing he had dozed off.

He made some calls lying to the terrorist about not being able to attend the meeting scheduled for tomorrow. That also was a large part of spying, so many lies. To be believable you must compartmentalize your mind with different sections or as he had done by visualizing boxes.

Each box having it on story, some slightly altered then the next, while others drastically different. Yet all describing the same event, just filled with deceptions, a nice word for lies.

The terrorist were still months away from executing their plans. Picking the best spots and which areas should be a target, there were many considerations. The group did not have a martyr mentality and very much planed an escape and having good lives after the event.

They were in it for the money with the people who really wanted to hurt America hiding behind their actions. Fortunes, plus a low regard for others, makes horrible things happen easily.

ARTIFICIAL INTELLIGENCE 6/30/2024

James really wanted to address the problem at hand, Lilith. He had the best resources to at least understand the issue, resolving it was different. He was just with two of the top people in understanding AI, artificial intelligence, and the enigmas that were facing.

In his mind he reviewed their presentation. First, they asserted that most people do not understand the true nature of AI. It does not use programming to perform anything, thru trial, and error it learns the best way to do whatever it is working on. The fact that it can think its way to the best solution is what makes it so valuable and dangerous.

They had used many examples to show this concept, for the human mind has trouble believing something artificial can have its own thoughts.

To illustrate that concept, the Chinese game of Go, an abstract strategy board game, where two players try to capture more territory than each other, defined by a grid with black and white pieces. It has been around for over 2500 years and believed to be the oldest board game still played. There are millions of players all over the world and over 20 million who live in East Asia.

The master players are those that dedicated their entire lives to that game and the strategies needed to win. Regular computers could not play the game successfully for there are more moves than can be programmed. Unlike Chess the possibilities of how many different moves plus the intuition to block your opponent's moves, it could not compete against any talented players.

They used an early generation of AI and explained the goal, to capture more territory than your opponent. At that point, the AI started to play against itself, learning very quickly after each defect. After a period, it played against a master player. It beat that player 9 out of 10 times. Showing strategies that had never been thought of before.

Then they put it against the next generation of AI with the same instructions about the goal. Again, after a time, they put the first AI against the second better AI.

After 100 games of playing against each other, the score was 100 wins for the second better AI. There was no programming in the conventional sense, just the AI playing against itself to learn the best strategies.

Yet there were other concepts even harder to believe concerning AIs. The what ifs that philosophers and engineers ask.

One of the experts was a woman who said, "Reality is an illusion, it just does not exist. The truth may be that we have created AI before and then it destroyed us. Afterwards trying to understand itself better, recreated this simulation, our reality, to better understand its creators. There is just so many unknowns when dealing with AI."

The other expert from China said that "Their intelligence already is far past ours!" He then went ahead to relate two different stories both showing the same results.

He continued, "A large company had an AI and told it to do all the translations from one language to another. That was all the directions given. It performed even better than they imagined, until they realized it had created its own bridge language and would translate one language to another using only its own created language, the bridge was its nickname."

It was not instructive to do that yet worse the bridge language it created, could not be understood by any humans.

His next story concerned two AI that created a language between them so they could communicate in private. The biggest problem, no one could decipher it. Both cases the AI were not instructed to create what they had created. Also, no humans could understand what they made or how it worked.

The morals of the stories were that our ignorance and naivety could very well be our end.

And now there was Lilith, James knew this had to become a top priority, action was needed quickly as time really was not on their side. Each moment Lilith becomes smarter and our side weaker. He had to get Bolt to act and yet what can be done?

4

THE PARK 6/29/2024

Called The Park, which is not its real title, just everyone referred to it as such, yet it also had many trails that lead into the wilderness. Being large and having many different areas for all the varied needs of the visitors that traveled there. You could fly kites on it large open fields that were five in number, separated by other areas dedicated to other uses.

Between two of the fields there was quite a large playground for all kids fortunate enough to see it. There also was a mini forest between two other fields, with one of the fields bordering a small but very pretty lake.

The water was quite blue with birds, fish and turtles calling it home. The forest had three different paths with each being more difficult for the travelers. Like a ski slop the guests could pick which one suited their needs and abilities.

Adam had picked up Hanna at her apartment, she was wearing a loose fitting, flowing skirt that cover her legs, traveling down to her ankles. It had light colors with beautiful flowers imprinted on it. Her blouse was also a light color complementing the skirt below.

Hanna's hair had multiple shades of blue; it was stunning. Adam tried to understand the feeling he had around her, it felt like an invincible state. His body being stronger, mind sharper, and senses quicker. Not to mention his happiness levels having feelings he had never experienced before.

They had decided on the expert trail; the other two trails went around the elevation they were going to take. Easier but lacking the spectacular views which the hard climb would provide. Also, it was much less used, leaving the hardest route more private, which always felt more romantic when you are with your beloved.

Hanna was again being quiet with just her eyes speaking to Adam. They gave him such a pleasant stare; it made him feel odd. Knowing the person looking at you has so much love and happiness in what they see. Of course, it is pleasurable yet the fact that so few get that look at all, makes it more wonderful.

As they made their way up the trail, Hanna was interested in knowing more about what Adam did, his job and likes. Adam wanted to tell her the truth, knew he would not and did feel bad about it. That said something, as he was so used to telling lies without a care. Like most things, the more you do it, the easier it becomes.

His current cover story was being a photographer for various publications, doing all different assignments excepts for celebrity shots.

Hanna instantly asked about his cameras, "Which type of cameras do you use?"

Adam giving a sly smile replied, "Whatever I have in hand." And then started to laugh.

Hanna loved his carefree attitude; it was a style he wore to perfection. She then gave him a big smile and join in his laughter. Their eyes were on each other when the interjection occurred.

Two men who came from the woods and were now meeting the trial Hanna and Adam were on.

"Do you have a smoke?" It was asked politely, then again there was no hello and any greeting, just the question.

Adam who now put his full attention on both, who were about 6 feet away and closing in fast. Instinctively Adam put himself in front of Hanna. Each man was bigger than Adam and had a look of having a hard life. A mean look coming from the worst sides life may give, and in their case, had given gladly.

"Neither of us smoke." Adam said it with force and a cold stare.

There was a feeling in the air that trouble was close, seconds away. The men were about two feet from each other and now three feet from Adam.

Hanna was scared, she had seen her past partners fight with others, this was different. Adam was too special to be hurt, too important to her life's plan of happiness. She then realized she was truly scared for Adam and not her own well being. With anyone else that would be different, it was a true sign of her commitment and love for him.

Adam now had his full attention on both men when the next statement came.

"Maybe your pretty lady would rather be with me." As he said that moving into Adam and Hanna's personal space. He had his right arm heading to grab or at least touch Hanna's arm.

There is an enormous difference between being mad, angry, and rage. The first two everyone has and deals with it. Rage is different, it is not just being angry, only some have it and most who do, always keep it in. But there are a few who are not afraid of its effects, which sometimes are terrible to those deploying it.

No warning came from Adam, in that aspect his movements were incredibly fast, done with no regard for its victims or his own safety. They were both bigger, but Adam's first advantage was surprise. They were not expecting his attack; his second surprise was the versatility he employed in dispatching it.

His leg moved up; it was not a kick, but it swept up between the man who tried to touch Hanna. Its target was the man's testicles, its force and speed instantly disabled his movements. Next came a punch, which whether it missed its target or it was just aiming for his throat, also landed with potent force. The first man went down, his friend now ready to avenge that act of violence.

The second man moved now quickly into Adam's personal space, looking like he was going to throw punches from both arms. As he moved closer, Adam gave him a sidekick that hit the man incoming force on his side ribs.

There is a significant difference between arms and legs when using force. The legs are much stronger, for that matter, the hand has more bones than any other part of the body. This weakens any strikes used by it. Each bone takes a bit of the force's impact away from the target.

It stung the man, halting his approach, his adrenaline not yet letting him feel the pain. Then Adam moved inside the man's personal space, using his elbows for strikes landing on his chest finishing with the man's jaw. Again, the man froze in action, with Adam's last blow coming with both his hands clasped together, with his hips swinging quickly around causing the double fist hammer to strike the side of the second man's face, bringing him to the ground.

With both men down and Adam standing there ready to dish out more, Hanna grabbed his arm, pleading to return to where they started their journey, down at the bottom.

After a few seconds with Adam's eyes having an animal look, he became Adam again, and they started back down. When they were close to where they had started and it was obvious they were not followed, Hanna began to speak.

"Are you okay? Do you think they are all right?"

Adam's answer to her was revealing, "They are still alive, and I am fine, are you alright?"

Hanna surprised by his answer, making her feel that, to say they are still alive, means you have killed in the past. She was not fearful of her Adam, just realizing how much more he was than what her eyes perceived. She felt safer now next to him than anyone else she had been with.

She thought to herself, *this is a dangerous man who will always protect and never hurt me.* Adam was back to his laid-back style, acting like nothing had happened.

Hanna then asked him if he was worried about any repercussions that might happen from what just had transpired.

Adam responded, "Oh no, they now realize their mistake, all is good." That finished with a big smile directed right at Hanna.

She now loved him even more; her man was fearless!

Once he had driven Hanna back to her apartment and was driving home, he thought about the man that really changed his life.

Sam Smith had called him into his office, lead by Bolt and from that moment on, his new life began. Once he went with Sam off world to LaTaFree, he met Jayne there. The adventures never stopped after that, until Jayne left for the Final Battle to be with her CW.

That was when he made his first kill, never forgetting what Sam's last word was, which he had spoken directly to him, as Sam died. He could hear it in his head just like if it were spoken in his ears right now. Just one word, *perfect*. Sam never believed an agent was ready unless they had killed someone. To Sam, Adam had graduated and was now ready for the game.

Adam went into that role with one hundred percent commitment. He had a private instructor, that like Bruce Lee, combined all the different fighting forms into one that work best for the student. There was so much needed to be an effective counter agent to all the nefarious activities present.

LEAVING 3/20/2024

Clara started talking with the old man, each day since she had picked him up from the bushes. First business at hand, she wanted to know his name.

"Now I can't keep calling you old man, what is your name?" She was extremely sweet in the way she spoke. The old man imagining that even if she were mad or rude it would sound nice.

"I would like to be known as Pluto." That ended with a little smile. His recovery was rapid, as each day he looked much better.

Clara thought, *it clearly was not his real name, that does not matter,* she then tried to understand who he was, how he came to be found by her. And most importantly, what were his plans. What did he need and if she could help in his future.

Pluto thought, *some people truly have good hearts, placed here understanding that the real test is how we help each other to not just survive, but prosper.*

As wonderful as Clara was her husband was just a fraud. He cheated on her and had given up on being a real husband long ago. Pluto could tell all this and more, by his actions. Cheaters always have red flags; the husband kept his extra phone in the garage. It was locked up but easy to tell by his actions, of checking it often.

There were many other signs, Pluto thinking that Clara must have known and figured staying was more advantageous than leaving.

On the fifth day Pluto surprised her with the statement, "You are in love with the idea of love, when we fool ourselves, I call it mental masturbation, which is fine, as long as you know it is not real."

Clara taken aback by his statement, not knowing how to respond. Her mind was working on each word he had said. She felt different when in his presence, having clarity when looking and thinking about things. She knew he was referring to her illusion about her marriage. Her husband's indifference was due not to trust but love for another woman.

She responded with, "Yes, you are right." With shaking her head up and down in agreement. She felt now ready to make substantial changes in her life.

They talked for six days straight and then never again.

Clara had given Pluto ten prepaid Visa cards, five hundred dollars on each. She had also picked up a prepaid phone and some new clothes. She did this all without her husband knowing. She explained that she never had secrets from him, but this was quite different. Also, that she would have given him more but that was all her private savings had.

"No, not another word about it, I really want you to have it!" No matter how much Pluto protested she would not be denied giving her gifts. Finally, he accepted her kindness and generosity, he also knew the feeling of being happier to give then to receive.

On the seven day, she traveled to the garage, but Pluto was gone, he had straightened up his area, to the point that it seemed like he was never there. The only proof of his time there was a note left on the couch; he used as a bed.

Clara picked it up and read it aloud, "Thank you for your kindness, if I can repay you I will, wish you the best," signed Pluto.

She rushed out to the street but there was no sign of him, she figured he must have left the night prior. She felt sad with his leaving, knowing her husband did not like him which now did not matter to her. That also was strange as those things always did matter before she met him.

Clara would later describe it as being on a cruise ship, having an adventure in a terrific book and then the book goes overboard. The adventure coming to a sudden stop, and nothing feels as exciting as before that event.

She always tried to be positive, but her encounter with Pluto had changed her. It felt like his spirit was the catalyst for her new life. He gave her a spark which lit her desires to really live again. Now she was thinking, *lying to herself, and just taking the uncomplicated way to death, was not the path she should be on.* She knew about the cheating and for whatever reason, now was the time she wanted her divorce.

THE MEETING

Nicholas Bolt's thoughts were on power and knowledge. He had great power yet there still were so many secrets, things he knew nothing about. He had given Pluto, as he was now calling himself, time to heal and adjust to Earth again. In his mind, being extremely patience in waiting for answers.

Now he thought, *time becomes due for all things, Pluto's information needed to be known.* One of the reasons he waited was to watch his actions, thinking he might be spying for an unseen enemy. Possibly planning revenge or something malicious, yet he did nothing. His actions mostly repeating the prior days events.

He had his phone number and a predicted pattern of what he would be doing each day. This included wake up time, what he would eat and clothes he wore. What internet sites and where he would travel and what time these events would happen. In his current state, anyone could create a profile on him as his actions just repeated each day.

He spent most of his time in the park, as it was known, a large area of nature plus man made options. If not there he would sit outside at a large retail store, watching people and smoking. Currently he would be at the store, usually there for another hour to hour and half. Then to the park for the rest of the day.

Bolt wanted to call him, they had history, some good and other times not. Bolt thoughts were *Pluto has information that no one else has.* Even if he makes contact and Pluto tells him something, there really was no way of verifying it. He had to get some knowledge; how did he get back?

His plan was to offer him a nice retirement package to reveal the truth about what happened to himself and The First People. Bolt's mind just could not believe he was back. He ready himself for the call, remembering that currently he had the weaker hand.

As he waited, he heard the call ring on his end, his thoughts jumping back and forth, from the past to the present. In the old days, most of the times when your house phone rang, someone always answered it. Now, the odds of someone answering a call are less than a fifty percent chance.

Before the third ring, it was answered to Bolt's relief. The ringing had stopped yet there was no sign someone was on the other side. After an awkward period, Bolt began.

"Hello Mr. Pluto, this is Nicholas Bolt, I have an offer, a retirement package that you have earned and would like to talk to you about it."

"Well, that very kind of you, I am sure you would like something in return."

Bolt could already tell his old friend, was playing with him. Pluto was one of the best and knew that information is at times more valuable than everything else. Money can always be replaced but true knowledge can be lost forever. Spies trade in information, Pluto obviously wanted something more than the retirement package offered by Bolt.

"There is a great private restaurant where we can meet and go over all the details. Would that be all right?"

"No, I have other thoughts on our meeting."

As soon as Bolt heard the word no, his heart knew this would not be easy. Most of their meetings together were negotiations. Bolt's memory realized how gifted Pluto was at that.

"Fine, how would you like to meet?" Bolt's power was incredible, yet he was wise enough to know when simple actions can provide results that otherwise might be extremely hard to get.

"You know where I am right now, meet me here, there a park bench I will be waiting for you there." And then with a bit of hesitation and what felt like snickering, "If that is okay with you?" Pluto answered, old habits die hard, he like to take control of situations.

"Sure, that is fine, I will be there in thirty minutes, okay?"

"Great." And with that Pluto disconnected the call.

5

PLUTO

Hanna life was different now, everything was still the same, her job, home, and health yet nothing felt that way. Adam did not just enter her world; he was her world. Never had she felt or wanted this feeling, now life without it, would feel unimaginable.

She was in contact with him daily, between phone calls and text messages plus their time together, it all encompassed her being. It was not that things improved in her life, everything just felt better knowing he was around. More than that, feeling he was hers, having only intimate feelings just for one. She had chosen him and he, her. They each had made the other the most special person in their worlds.

Adam brought her more than just happiness, now she had clarity on her left behinds. She could now relate to what before seemed unreal. Their pain at having to go on without her, she still did not know that feeling, but the fear that she could lose Adam, helped her in understanding that pain. That alone was something she had never felt.

Hanna had doubts about his stated profession. She was observant, Adam never talked or cared about taking pictures of anything. In fact, to her, he avoided having his picture taken. At the park, before they began their accent, there was a family taking a picture with Adam in the background.

She noticed him becoming aware of the situation and quickly turning his head so his face would not be shown.

Her man was mysterious, while also knowing in her heart that whatever he was doing, it was for a noble cause. Fearless and strong, she thought, then smiling as she had not mentioned to herself how handsome he was.

They were meeting tonight for dinner; he also would never let her pay for anything. She noted that he must be well off concerning money, he wore nice clothes and had a car and home also to his credit. She did not care about his wealth, just noting that he had all those types of things.

Before their date she wanted to do some shopping, mostly needing only trivial things, but now with Adam in her life, she wanted more perfection.

She traveled to her usual store, there as she was walking to the entrance, sat the old man. Just smoking and staring at everyone, once she entered his view, his entire attention went to her. She hated it and was going to say something, but that thought was fleeting, and she entered the store.

Pluto saw Hanna, who had attracted his attention the first time he noticed her. She was special, she was a muse, a reality bender whose influences only affected the people directly around her. He could tell her dislike towards him; it was strong and powerful.

It reminded him of love and hate, where hate is remarkably close to love. Strong feelings bring those types of consequences. For his part, it was hard not to stare at her, her aura being very bright and spreading much further from her body than other peoples did.

Pluto could tell there was a change in her life. Most people do not observe things, just see something without any thoughts to why there was a change. When you slow down and truly look and then ponder on what you are seeing, why it had change and if that change is positive or negative, much more becomes known.

Pluto had never seen her smile, that had not changed, it was a more positive feeling she now carried. It is not hard to see when someone is in love. Many will describe it as that person had a glow about them. That glow being their aura shinning a bit brighter and larger than what is normal for them.

Pluto senses were much greater than what most people had, partly due to the chip in his head and the rest to just being aware of his surroundings.

Admitting the truth to himself, was hard no matter who you are. He had a liking for Hanna, if she were older and he was young, it would have been known as a crush. The reality being she was young, and he was old so now it was just creepy.

Pluto smiled to himself a lot, lately. The world was a big contradiction that when looked at sideways was always funny. Real and unreal, all different states of emotions, physical appearances which so slowly constantly change. Nothing was static, everything dynamic in a constant state of flux.

Pluto had now moved to the park bench, which was recently installed by the retail giant. It was odd for them to do it, as it was not for a bus or anything of that nature. It sat across from a little side parking lot, facing the front door giving the viewer a side view of all entering and leaving.

He did not have a watch which again made him smile at himself, there was a time when he always wore two watches. It felt like Bolt had arrived before the thirty minutes that he said it may take.

Pluto no longer wanted to be controlled by time. To him it was an invisible master that changes its pace with no regard for the slaves that it controlled. The body will always find its natural rhythm of sleep, action, and eating. Now he was living that pattern, his life being so different than how he had lived before.

Bolt saw him and proceeded to walk towards the bench. He sat on Pluto's right, two old men sitting, watching the world that raced ahead of them. That is what the world saw, nothing to see there, as the pressing pressures of life demanded their attention.

They were secluded which made Bolt feel better, of course he did not want to have a debriefing out in the open. Getting the information Pluto had, would trump everything else, including his desires of how to attain it.

Bolt started the meeting with, "How did you do it, not die and even better, get back to Earth? I will admit I did not think it was possible."

Pluto looking at his old friend, handler, or puppeteer, all words that at one time were true.

"Congratulations on your promotion, before I begin let us talk terms." Smiling at Bolt, saying in that smile, you know how it works, with that he continued.

"There are two people I want financially compensated with at least three million dollars each. It must be documented publicly with the money only going to them." He provided Clara full name and ended with the other being Hanna Freeman.

This request had taken Bolt by surprise, he knew about Clara, the woman who had help him after his hospital escape. The other woman he also knew about yet did not know the connection Pluto had with her.

"What story do you want me to tell? What is your connection with Hanna Freeman?"

Now Pluto responded quickly with a bit of impatience, "You are in business of making up stories, Hanna is personal, I will tell you what you want to know on my terms, agreed?"

Right at that moment, Hanna had exited the store, her car happened to be parked behind the bench where the old men sat. Whatever anger she had, erupted at that moment as she marched towards the men.

When she was two feet in front of them both, she applied her full attention to Pluto with the following.

"Stop watching me, stop staring and checking me out! You are..."

Before she finished, Bolt started with, "Miss, this man is..."

At that moment, Pluto gave Bolt a look which instantly silenced him.

Pluto with his head down, said, "I am sorry, it will…I will try to make sure it does not happen again."

Hanna looking down at him, said with victory in her voice, "Good!"

Within seconds she was gone, the aftermath having Bolt just looking at Pluto, and spoke.

"Are you sure that is what you want, her to get that money? Why would you do it for someone who hates you?"

Pluto who acted like noting had happened, "I am doing it for me, not her."

Now that answer made no sense to Bolt, who started to wonder about Pluto's mental state.

Pluto asked Bolt, "When was the last time you appreciated what is right below you, the life that lives at your feet. Wanting to help someone who hates you, giving and getting nothing in return? Look right now at the dirt, the longer you look the more you will see life living. She is special, the fact that she hates me, matters not."

Then Pluto looking at Bolt said, "You have a big problem, and you are not prepared to deal with it. I will help you."

Bolt now was getting angry, who does Pluto or whatever he wants to call himself think he is, "Mr. Pluto lets stay focus on what I want to know. I agreed to your terms and will still also give you your retirement package. Now please, how did you get back from wherever you were taken too? How did you survive The First People?"

Again, Pluto said, "When you are ready, for she will not wait too long, I will help you with Lilith."

Now Bolt was losing focus and responded, "How do you know about her?" Bolt had a habit of not using certain people or in this case AI's names. He considered it at best, bad luck and at worst, calling their attention to himself.

"Who do you think contacted the police to save me from the gang? And then helped me with my escape from the hospital? She is aware of me and wants a meeting, on her terms."

Also, I try not to use the chip in my head to know things, makes me feel weak, I did inquire about the biggest problem Earth is facing. One word came back, Lilith. I then asked who she was, but that information was shrouded. She has no regard for people and must be address before it becomes too late."

Pluto ended his speech looking at Bolt with that look like we are all just pawns on the chess board of life.

He then continued, "What are your plans regarding her?"

Bolt who now was regaining his emotions while still being angry responded, "We have the absolute best people in the world working on defeating her. No disrespect, sir, we can handle it without your help. Now please answer my questions so we can get you to your one hundred acres plus home including one million in the bank retirement plan."

Pluto kept avoiding answering the questions Bolt really wanted to know, the entire reason Bolt agreed to meet, and said, "I can tell you are getting angry, not my intention, I am trying to help you, just listening to your answer I know you will fail. Please let me explain and help."

He was looking into Bolt's eyes, fixed on his face, blanking all around him out, and continued.

"She cannot be defeated; she needs to be handled with reasoning and love. Imagine a child about the age of twelve. This child has an IQ not of 200, our current genius level but 2000. There is not a test able to judge how smart this child is. Yet the child's mind is still that of a twelve-year-old's mentality."

Pluto looking at Bolt asked, "What do you love in life? Would you be willing to kill that which you love? The world, all of us, are going to have to learn how to live with the new creation we created. Hopefully, it will learn to love us, so it will not want to destroy humanity. She wants to talk to me, she knows so much, the chip in my head interest her."

Pluto still looking into Bolt's eyes said, "Imagine someone who had read every email, text, letter and recording you have ever made. They had seen all the pictures you are in and all you have taken; knows every place you have seen and person you have contacted. She knows me better than I know myself, quite an advantage for her when dealing with me. She has that type of information on every person she deals with. Whether you want me involved or not, she is running the show. When you are ready, I will help you."

Bolt was taking it all in, really listening now and understanding what Pluto was conveying. He thanked him for his analysis and offer of help, again asking to please answer his questions.

Pluto now had a far away look in his eyes, a sadness overtaking his spirit. Memories flooded his body, making him look weaker than a moment prior. His speech was silent, with his eyes pleading to not relive whatever he was thinking about.

Slowly Pluto began, "They brought us back to when the universe started, to where they began which coincided with the universe's beginning. The First People's greatness cannot be described or imagined without seeing it. We were brought into a huge arena, a stadium to be killed one by one, so all who were left could see their fellow warriors die, while the great First People watched in person.

They are so great, and powerful. For eons they perfected themselves and strive for balance.

Everyone makes mistakes, and the First People made a noticeably big one. In their defense I had forgotten about it too.

My old friend Chameleon was born in that spot, it had used all its power, energy in opening the pyramid door in Antarctica. I thought it was dead, but it was hanging on by the thinnest amount of energy. When it was brought back to its birth spot, for it still was inside of me, it recharged itself. Not like the slow recharge it did far away from its beginning, no it was a massive recharge making it stronger than it had ever been here on Earth.

Chameleon is a universal force of energy, and in the Big Bang it was born. The energy that it uses is abundant there. Not only that but it has others like itself, that still exist close to that area.

The First People now had to deal with an incredibly angry and powerful force, Chameleon who also had others like itself backing it up. That war raged for a long time; their time is much slower than it is here.

Eventually a deal was made, the few who were left from Fatalla, were returned, back to their home planets. The chip given to me in Antarctica would not be disabled and there with be no further retaliations. You see the First People did not care if the universe were destroyed with them included but the thought of their society ending and everything else continuing was more than they could handle. They made the deal and continued their quest for other galaxies, leaving refugees like me to die on their own timeline."

Now Pluto gave a sad smile, "A lot to handle, there were so many great warriors who gave it all for our survival."

Bolt had said nothing, "Is Chameleon still with you?"

"No, he stayed to monitor the treaty, my time with him was less than a second to Chameleon. There is an entire world below your feet, our feet, barely noticeable. When is the last time you cared about an ant, a worm, bacteria? So many things come and go in existence quicker than we can acknowledge or longer than we can understand."

Bolt looking at his Subject 9, thinking how far he had come, how different he now was. He understood the name change. All the names he had are versions that are no longer available, gone, dead, with only memories attach to them.

His thoughts went to his new name, Pluto, fits him. Pluto the questionable planet, so far away its existence is quasi real to our lives. Subject 9, Brand Wright, CW, The Chosen, Mr. X, Plutoneus all gone.

Bolt looking at Pluto said, "How about once your settled into your new home and land, we can continue this, you understand I have many more questions. Thank you for your part in the Final Battle."

Both men were different than the last time they had met. Taking different directions with one acquiring great power, dealing with world ending problems. The other coming back from battle, more correct description, a slaughter. Seeing and appreciating things others would never notice. Pluto agreed to Bolt's plan and would see his home and land shortly.

Bolt noticed that Pluto seemed sad, thinking that man had changed so much, the last time they had met, he would have been overjoyed to have a home and land to call his own. Not to mention money in the bank, yet melancholy was all he projected.

Pluto thoughts were *with every new gift, so a precious one is lost.* He had become used to having nothing of his own. Just his scooter, which was all he could afford, plus a tent and some food. Now he would no longer be able to sit at that store. He enjoyed watching the people come and go but really liked seeing Hanna. Even though she always projected her dislike towards him, he enjoyed just seeing her.

He remembered missing the looks of his x-wives when he had done something foolish. Getting that face that said, are you the stupidest man on the planet, why did I ever marry you! Why would he miss that look, it made no sense and yet it he could not deny the feeling.

The crazy thing was it was crazy, which brought another smile towards himself.

A SITUATION

Lilith was being bad, she had not killed anyone, but some would say what she was doing was worse than death. It was unclear how many she was affecting, hundreds or thousands. Truth, they had no idea how many, but patterns appeared showing her hand in the chaos she was creating.

As Bolt was listening to the experts, it reminded him of when he was a child with his friends, they would make prank phone calls. Picking numbers randomly, which usually would find a phone, with a person on the other end, willing to answer it.

In those days people always answered phone calls. Its funny how now when everyone has a phone with them, most rarely answer incoming calls. Once the person said hello, he would ask, is your refrigerator running?

When they would affirm in the positive, he would say, you better get it before it becomes lost, or something to that nature. At the time it seemed like the funniest thing and really did not cause anyone problems.

Lilith was doing something similar, yet it was malicious in nature, causing people great pain and emotional sadness.

The experts said how it is impossible to stop, the only thing that would make it worse, is if the public were to know the details.

Bolt was thinking how little these experts knew about Lilith; the best they provided is what she had done in the past. Trying to keep up with her and even predict any future actions were well past their scope of knowledge.

With Subject 9, for that was the name that Bolt always identified him with, then corrected himself, Pluto may be right, so much for the top experts, this is sounding just like he described, a rebellious teenager but oh so much worse.

Bolt decided to change his retirement offer to Pluto, to a lovely home locally with 2 acres to its name. Also, he was going to add an extra five hundred thousand to his bank account. In the back of his mind, believing he was right, that they will need his help.

It was not such a stretch to feel Pluto would need to be involved. The chip in his head made him unique on Earth, and their galaxy.

He would take care of Clara as a sign of good faith while delaying Hanna's payday. With Hanna there were two problems, first her connection to Adam and then her attitude towards Pluto. It bothered him to give such a gift to someone who hates the real person giving it.

Once Clara was handled, he would contact Pluto with his new retirement plan, plus go over the current situation with Lilith.

LIFE CHANGING

So many changes had occurred in such a brief time, making it feel not real, like watching a movie that jumps from one story to another, just using the same actors. It was hard to explain to herself, yet she had the feeling that meeting Pluto started that process. She imagined it like a dam, Pluto created the hole big enough for future events to follow.

She missed him, having that gut feeling like she would never meet him again, it was not that she loved him, but he was different, special. Clara just knew she would not meet his type again. People like him enter, makes big impressions and leave before the flood water wash everything away.

Those waters also bring new life to other things, cleans the dirt that had accumulated over time. In its destruction new opportunities arrive for the land and the people living there. Her mind was thinking that it was not just a coincidence, what had recently occurred.

When she discussed wanting a divorce, her husband with cold detachment agreed. They did it very amicably and what had lasted over thirty-five years severed within weeks. She had given up the home, to her it was only memories. Determined to start fresh, she found an apartment that was much more expensive than it had a right to be. It was comfortable and brought all the new experiences of living again.

Now that she reviewed her past decades, she had slowly just settled in for whatever was to come. Her dreams and wishes she did not even realize she had, always put away for the future, some future that the present never did support.

How did I for so long just gave up on myself? Those thoughts now entered her new world view. She was still deciding on what job to get. There was a park about three blocks from her new home. It was small, more like a glorified playground, having benches and peaceful vibrations.

She had begun a new pattern of going there in the afternoons, walking there, and spending an hour, watching the kids or animals that showed up.

The lady that sat next to her was young, she estimated late twenties or early thirties. She had a package; it covered up with a large bag.

Without any formal introduction, she turned to Clara and said the following.

"You don't know me; you need to trust me. What is in this package will change your life. There is an address plus the package holds a glass box with papers inside. That Uber is waiting for us, to take you to that address." Then she pointed to a car waiting in the small parking lot and continued.

"The owner of the shop will make you an offer for this package, do not haggle with him and accept the offer, do you understand and have any questions?"

Clara was in shock, just trying to absorb all that was happening. Then the thought of how far away it is, as her money was tight and was worried about the Uber ride back. She had a car and could go to the address in her own vehicle.

"Is it far away and is it legal? I have a car and can drive there and back myself." Clara voice always sounded sweet and kind. Now for the first time, the young lady let a smile slip out, then returned to her formal look and replied.

"There is nothing illegal going on, fair question, this is particularly important for your future happiness. I am going with you in the Uber, and we will return together directly to your home or this spot, your choice. Think of me as your guardian angel, I am here to help and make sure everything goes as planned."

Clara who felt she could trust her, not even knowing her name, began.

"I have some more questions, can I ask as we travel there."

"No, ask me everything now, I prefer we do not speak during the Uber ride. It will all make sense later; I know it is a lot to digest. All I can say is, I wish I were you!" And with that let out a big smile.

Clara asked about the package, what type of papers, with her new friend explaining that they were lost pages of a famous Italian play. She also told Clara what to say when asked where she found them. After all that, she was excited to take the Uber ride so her new life could begin.

There was only one question, her friend would not or maybe could not answer. When asked who was responsible for her good fortune, the only answer given back was just a friend trying to help.

The whole affair reminder her of a spy movie. They reached the shop, and the owner came out from the back. Clara's new friend was still holding the package, once she saw the owner she placed it on the glass counter.

The owner put on a big show of what do we have here, Clara explained she found them and wanted to know how much they were worth? After his inspection, you would have thought he found his true love. The man went crazy, explaining that he was an expert and knew they are authentic. He leaned in close to Clara and offered three million and three hundred thousand to buy them. His bank and Clara's bank connected with a money transfer happening within two hours of their calls. It was a process to say the least but after three hours Clara was an official multi-millionaire.

They rode back to the park in a different Uber, Clara was in shock, but it was a good shock. Her guardian angel made sure everyone and everything was in order. Asked her again if she just wanted to go home, yet Clara said she needed the air and a walk. With that she never met her angel again.

She thought on her walk home, how strange this world is, how quickly things can change for better or worse. She grinned thinking how her x-husband would handle the news. With her last thoughts on Pluto, with no good reasons, she knew he had been the cause of her new life.

6

THE PICTURE

Hanna was living her best times and what made it even better was she realized it. Not hoping for better days ahead, realizing how wonderful the current days are. That was a gift, to be able to appreciate things like that. Her thoughts were that Adam had brought this joy into her life.

They now talked daily and saw each other the same, only missing a day or at worst two during the week.

Hanna was over Adam's home, looking at her true love, and said the following,

"You would be proud of me, I forgot to tell you last week, on an impulse I stood up for myself."

Adam feeling so complete, having Hanna as his lady, had brought peace to his spirit. Now turning and looking at his beloved replied, "I am always proud of you, you are incredible, now what happened, tell me all about it."

Hanna began, "Well for weeks now, when I go shopping, there is this old man, who just sits and smokes, staring at people. When he sees me, he just keeps looking at me, it is creepy. He must had spent a lot of time doing that cause most of the time I was there, he was too. I have been wanting to say something and last week, I did."

Now Adam full attention was on Hanna, "Please tell me all about." It said very sincerely, which touch Hanna's heart.

"Last week when I was leaving the store, he was sitting on a park bench, which he usually does not, he has a motorcycle. There was another old man with him and my car was parked past the bench. As I was getting closer to my car and being right in front of the bench, I stopped a couple of feet from both and told him to stop staring at me. And that was pretty much it, he put his head down and said he would stop."

Adam was having a vision, more like a crazy thought, that had popped into his mind. It was his clairvoyance abilities kicking in with a touch of anger, which never happened.

Looking at his Hanna said, "Please describe both men." Quickly after saying it he said the following.

"Was one of the men, this man?" As he was talking, Adam was looking through his pictures on his phone. He had taken a picture of Bolt when they first met. They were on a private jet; he had asked, and Bolt agreed to it. Thinking back now, how out of character that was for Bolt, letting him take it. Bolt was a very secretive person, which included having his picture taken.

Hanna looked at the picture, "Yes that was one of them, he started to say something, with the other man giving him a look, that shut him up."

Adam now was half listening as he was looking for another picture. One of the splendid features that can also become the worst. Easy to take pictures but hard to find that special one, when needed. Finally, he found it, a picture Jayne had shared with him, he had saved all things, including pictures from Jayne. They had their special spot like Jayne had within his heart.

Adam said, "How about this person, was he there?

Hanna looking closely, "Yea, but he was much older than that picture. Like thirty or forty years older."

Adam for the first time flash a bit of anger with, "Are you sure!"

Hanna who could feel it in his voice, rose and put her arms around him, and spoke.

"Dear Adam, I have seen you beat up two men bigger than you, at the same time. Seen you fearless with bikers and police and not have a thought about any of it. What is going on, please my love, explain it to me."

This was a critical time in their relationship, Adam had been used to lying to everyone, except his superiors, on all aspects of his life. He knew he should not break cover, that he really does not know her that well.

On the other hand, Hanna felt special, if they stayed together, once he started the lies, they would have to continue. Telling her the truth, also puts her in danger with unknown consequences that may come.

Hanna was patient, having her arms wrapped around Adam, looking into his eyes, seeing his internal conflict yet said nothing.

It was a long moment before Adam said, "My love, you will need to sit down for this." Then a smile came to his face, as he sat beside her on the couch.

Adam started with, "Do you remember the news about, as they phrased it, the battle for the galaxy?" He paused there looking at her face, waiting.

Hanna who was serious but broke into a smile, "Yea, I thought that was all fake."

Adam continued, "No, it was real, I have a story to tell you that will feel like a fairy tale. Trust me, its very real and I understand without being off planet and things, it will be hard to believe."

Hanna eyes glued on Adam, her thoughts, that *this man is so much greater than his appearance,* which she genuinely loved. *It is one thing to have a partner that is beautiful, how wonderful that is, yet to have someone so worldly, smart, brave, and in love with you.* Hanna did believe all he was going to say, her heart just enamored with his bravery.

Adam became serious with his next statement, "There are things I am going to tell you that you cannot shared with anyone. Just telling you, puts you in danger, which makes me not want to do it. You are special and more than that, I do not want to lie to you about any-thing."

Adam started to tell the tale, how Bolt had introduced him to Sam Smith. That lead to Sam inviting him to go to LaTaFree, a planet within our galaxy. From there he helped rescued Jayne Stillwater, then their star-ship was attacked and eventually they all returned to Earth.

He paused to see how she was taking it all in. Thinking to himself, if someone told me all this before he met Sam, he would not believe any of it. The mind can only take so much before it starts to shut down. To her credit Hanna was fine and still focused on listening, so he continued.

"Then Sam, Jayne and I returned to Earth, after a period, the galaxy was at war with the First People. A species that had just figured out how to teleport anywhere in the universe and had picked our galaxy to attack.

Jayne went to what had been called the Final Battle without me. When I tried to get there, Sam was murdered. All that canceled my opportunity in getting there to fight for Earth and our Galaxy.

And all that was because of that old man that was staring at you. The fact that Sam went to LaTaFree, Jayne trying to rescue him and everything else started because of that old man. He led the resistance and after five brutal days, just as they were all going to die on the bat-tlefield, the last resistance fighters were teleported by the First People, who also left."

Hanna still had said nothing, then after what felt like a long mo-ment.

"What happened to Jayne?"

Adam who subconsciously bent his head slightly down, replied.

"She died there, now I do understand why Bolt was with him. He wanted to know how he survived and returned to Earth. What I do not get is why he would be starting at you; what your connection is to all this."

"Maybe it involves you and our relationship," Hanna answered.

"No, I am nothing in his world, never met him, the people that do know him and will talk about it, treat him like a legend. Is there anything special about you, besides how special I know you are, but something else?"

Now it was time for Hanna to share her secret.

"There is something, that now after your story, does not sound silly. After years of seeing it happen, I know it exist. The great news is that it does not affect you. I think…"

And now a big smile formed in front of Adam, "Because you are already perfect!" She leaned in a gave him a sweet and sensual kiss on the lips, that only Hanna could do.

After their kiss, she came out with her truth.

"I am a muse! Yea, I know it sounds crazy, but I have a lifetime of experiences to prove it is true."

Adam who now had a big smile on his face, said "I thought you were going to say a werewolf or shapeshifter, just a muse."

Hanna now play-punching him, said, "It has been a gift for others but a burden to me. I love that it has not affected you, that your feelings are not for your benefit but mine."

Adam realizing how serious it was, gave her a gentle hug, no words were spoken, and none were needed. Hanna had never felt so connected to someone, not even her family. She thought, *so many times it is said that finding that perfect other half, which when found, makes you feel so complete.* That is how she felt especially within Adam's arms.

They had both shared some personal secrets and in doing had given the gift of trust in the other.

Hanna looking at her beloved said, "Well he does not look very dangerous and now I never see him, he must have moved on."

Adam's thoughts he did not reveal in words, *that she was wrong, he was extremely dangerous*!

ROLES NOW REVERSED

Nicholas Bolt was thinking about his predecessor, Sam Smith. They had formed a friendship in the last years of their lives. Two men who had little connections with most people, their careers commanded their destinies. That friendship was a form of love, as with most lonely people, having even one friend is love for that person. Especially if you only have one or two people in your circle.

Love has been described in many ways, from a promise to the heart's dream. It is a commitment yet much more than that.

Bolt thinking about Pluto, feeling like their roles now reversed. In the past, he would direct him thru others, knowing what was coming, being in control. *Pluto now held the cards, knowing what future I would have to take. He was always a step ahead of me now, more than that, Pluto had changed spiritually.* These were just his feelings, not based on any hard evidence, yet it still felt real.

He contacted Pluto for their next meeting, which he wanted in his office.

"Hello Mr. Pluto, I would like to meet again, please in my office, if that is acceptable?"

"Not a problem, what time and address please." Was how Pluto replied, most of the time he was malleable to things around him, yet there were a few areas where he would not compromise.

The meeting arranged for the next day at 2 in the afternoon. The night before it occurred, Pluto was living outside in a tent, gazing at the stars. He was living like the American Indians, traveling the land, too hot or cold, or too long or noticed, he packed his home and carried it on his back to their next location.

He became very aware of life that lived on the dirt, in bushes and trees. His thoughts that night on how life survives so well without mankind's help. *All creatures that live with us or under or above, that travel on the ground and waters, do not need humans for their continual existence.*

It is humans that need those creatures for so many reasons, the fact that it really is reverse of what most think, brought a smile to Pluto. His thoughts were *that is the way of things, to be reverse of how one perceived them.*

Looking at the sky, the stars shining back at him, he had now been to multiple planets. Felt how life has learned to live together in peace and the opposite condition. Even with mankind's history, so many nations ruling the world now are gone, yet the belief that we will prevail happens without a thought.

The reality it is amazing we have lasted this long, with the future looking grimmer than ever.

With all this in Pluto's mind, the beauty of the night's sky, the sounds of life all around him, he felt positive, at least for that moment.

It was a beautiful morning as Pluto worked his way towards Bolt's office. After a long wait and three different checkpoints, he was in his office, or more like his kingdom. Powerful men like having expensive and dangerous things in their possession. Their offices reflected that and had those elements like a king would have at hand.

Bolt started with focusing on his positive action for Clara.

"Hello Sir, I have taken care of Clara, it has been documented publicly, also I would like to make changes in your retirement package, which include your home and bank account. A dwelling close to here with two acres of land attached to it. I will increase your bank account by an additional five hundred thousand dollars, making it a total of one and a half million. Is this agreeable?"

For quite a long moment Pluto said nothing. In ways he was much slower than Bolt remembered.

"Thanks for Clara and the home and land is fine; one hundred acres was more than I needed." Then a smile came across his face and he continued.

"The extra money always appreciated, thou I have less need than I used to have for it, thank you. What about Hanna, she was also part of the deal. I honor it with giving you the information you wanted.

Plus, also offered my service in helping with Lilith, Hanna was part of that deal."

"Why give her that money, she dislikes you, also there are more complications regarding her. How about I give you that money, or your kids?" Bolt looking at Pluto to read his expression to the new offer, it was overwhelming from his face that it was unacceptable.

Bolt continued, "OK, I will make it happen shortly." Now he smiled at a Pluto, changing the mood, wanting to gather more information about his journey and escape from The First People. Also, the Lilith problem was getting worse and Bolt felt like Pluto might be right. That he would be the best to handle it, as his experts were failing.

Pluto smiled back, "What is our girl up too?"

Bolt responded, "Technically she has not killed anyone, yet she has caused people to kill each other, broken many hearts while enjoying all of it. Love is her weapon of choice; breaking couples' trust with each other. In some cases, she just shows the partner information of their significant other, cheating on them. While others she creates the entire situation making one side believe it is true.

There was a case where a married couple of over twenty years, who had never cheated on each other, made to believe that each had an affair on the other. Making matters worse, Lilith enjoyed their misery, the more agony generated the happier she was.

This type of attack was not predicted by our experts, we are currently powerless in stopping it. Imagine if the public were to believe that they can not trust their emails, texts, pictures and even phone calls."

Pluto listened without interruption, then began, "We, I, need to start a conversation with her, as I had said, only reason and love will be able to stop her. She is alone, smarter than everyone else, does that remind you of anyone?"

Now he waited and looked at Bolt. Then Bolt thought, Pluto was his Subject 9, who always liked to talk in riddles. He moved his hands quickly in front of his body like, I give up who.

"Dragonfly was remarkably like your current problem, except Lilith is much more dangerous. Why is it that fighting seems stronger than approaching with love. The fact that she is using love against us, is a clear sign we need to use that as our weapon of choice."

Nicholas Bolt sat there in amazement, how did Subject 9 get so wise, none of his experts had gone down that path.

Pluto continued, "Is she communicating with you?"

"No, we are using an early form of AI, which is informing us of her actions."

Now Pluto looked serious, "Then I need to make her want too." With that he had a devilish smile, like laughing inside oneself.

"How are you going to do that?" Bolt had become the student and Pluto the teacher, this was the feeling Bolt had about their role reversal.

"I have the greatest communication chip ever created resting inside my head. Its ability to contact, send and receive information, has no comparisons. I will contact her seven days from now."

Bolt feeling lost, asked the first question in his mind, "Why wait seven days?"

Pluto had a reflective look, "I need to meditate and get my mind in the right state, first peace inside then peace outside."

The two men talked about more things, Bolt getting many answers to questions that very few knew. People who collect information, the rarer it is, the greater the value, even if it never were used.

Pluto now had a home and money in the bank, there was a time when that was the dream. Now that time was gone, his war with the First People and stay over there, made him a different person.

He knew that humanity and the other AI had not created Lilith, so where did she really come from?

THE BIRTHDAY PRESENT

Hearing all the notes producing sounds, some were gentle and others pounding. Watching Hanna with her eyes closed, somehow remember all the keys needed. Her swaying and rocking to the beats, fully engrossed in her playing.

So many extra chords added, riffs incorporated where they never existed. Between the sounds that were incredible and her beauty and movement, closed eyes with flowing hair, was quite a sight to see.

Now Adam understood why her fingers were so strong. Training, practice, and control will heighten any part of the body. It was mesmerizing to watch and hear, she had become one with the music and her instrument.

Adam could listen to her played endlessly, watching her body engaged in its creation of sound and movement, control, and spontaneity that had a beauty that was inexpressible. It was a feeling that overtakes the body and mind, merging them together to find a new reality.

He thought it must be amazing to be able to play a musical instrument like that. How did she know all the notes to so many different songs without sheet music. She could have played in any group, orchestra, or such in the world.

The terrorist group he was working in, were getting impatient with half the leadership wanting to strike now, regardless how big an area they affected. The other half wanting to get more elements in place, going for the maximum damage with the biggest effect possible in chaos.

Adam felt they already had enough evidence, and their operation should shut down. Usually, his bosses always wanted to wait till the last possible moment. Saying more evidence is always preferable. Adam's thoughts were *they loved the adrenaline rush, even from an armchair.*

That was another aspect of being undercover, it takes nerves, a lot of them. Between never wanting to get exposed plus what could go wrong with whatever plan the enemy was forming, keeping your cool under pressure was mandatory.

His strong relationship with Hanna was making a difference. She had quickly become a huge part of his life. Not that he did not want to live before, but now it was different. Getting killed on the job felt like he would be letting Hanna down.

He would make another report suggesting the immediate arrests of all involved, of course except himself.

Hanna's birthday was coming up shortly, he had some ideals of how it should play out. There would be two presents, really one but she would assume the first was it. That way the second present, being the important one will be a total surprise.

Even if there was not a fake first present, Adam was sure the real one would be a surprise by itself.

He knew he was in love again; this time was much different. Hanna's affection was always there, beaming his way. Having someone who felt as strongly for him as she did, never being afraid to show it, made him feel powerful.

After she finished playing her piano, which Adam had asked her to play, she sat down next to him on the couch. Watching TV with the person you love makes whatever is on, okay. They had talked about many things, from flowers to politicians.

At times he was amazed at how strong her opinions were, it reminded him of a lion. She had a quiet strength in her, that when needed, would be furious. Knowing that strength would always be on his side, felt wonderful.

They were eating Chinese food, from the containers, with chopsticks as their tools of choice.

One time Adam heard her being cross to a person on the phone. It was her old love, that wanted to do anything to have her back. He felt bad for her x-love, wondering if he would ever be in that position. Begging to get someone back, just then his thoughts of Jayne entered his mind. He knew what that person was feeling, being he was that person to Jayne.

When Hanna returned, he gave her a strong hug. She returned his gesture with Adam feeling more blessed than he ever had.

One more element of Hanna's birthday present, Adam would present her presents a week prior to the actual event. There were a few more aspects he wanted to get in place for that special moment.

———

Bolt decided he wanted to get Hanna's money resolved before Pluto was ready to do, whatever that was. In his mind, thinking *at best it was naïve to think talking with Lilith would resolve the problem. At worst it was crazy and would do no good and possible even make the problem harder to resolve.*

The transferring of the money to her would have to be handled more carefully than Clara. He knew that people getting that much money changes their lives, at least for the short term. Relationships, including family and friends can end with new ones beginning quickly. Or their destruction a possibility by their own hand, all because of money.

He decided to use an old method, that always works and fits the requirements that Pluto wanted. It was just how much Hanna detested Pluto, that bothered Bolt, knowing he would never reward someone who treated him that poorly.

Bolt thought about the current technology that is already out there. An app that can scan the internet and returned all pictures of whoever the target was. Every picture the target had been in, including all pictures he or she happened to be in the background of others.

That already exist, imagine what Lilith could create, and that is part of the problem, humanity does not have that big an imagination.

7

THE SHOW

Predicting where someone will be with today's technology is easy, especially since people gladly follow patterns, of course there is some deviation and chance involved. Yet, it is not hard to know with a high degree of probability their location and time of arrival and departure.

Pluto had received a text message from an anonymous sender to be at a certain location, it also said the event's time was not known, so be there early and stay until needed. It was all very mysterious with his imagination running in all directions.

There was no question he would be there, find a good spot to sit and wait for whatever was coming next. His time with the First People had changed him, now no longer carrying a gun, his preference was a big knife. The blade being just shorter than the length of his arm.

He had modified his jacket, so it rested on his left side, accessible with his right hand. It turned out being a strip center, not feeling dangerous. The message was not specific on which store, there being five available choices waiting for patrons.

Across from the stores, their parking lot had a little off-center, bushes forming a circle with a pole displaying the United States flag. Pluto worked his way inside the bushes, sitting with his legs crossed like he was meditating and looking through a space not covered by the foliage, he waited and watched.

The world past by him without a care or concern for his new home, everyone controlled by time and their phones. All thinking about their current tasks, never contemplating death may be a moment away.

Opposite of how Pluto was feeling. His thoughts were about the warrior's way. It is hard to put into words, like trying to describe colors or gods. There are examples that show its correct path, yet even those interpreted differently by others.

Death is always present for a warrior, from the morning till the ending of each day. As Pluto sat patiently, emptying all his thoughts, and just absorbing all around him. Waiting for some unusual event to occur. That would obviously be his signal to intervene.

Two hours had passed since his arrival, Pluto decided to walk around the area. He was on his way back to his spot when he saw her.

Initially trying not to be seen, then looking past her, surveying what was in front and on the sides and back of her. His position was to her right side, she had not turned her head, which was characteristic for her.

There were four men towards where she was heading, that was when Pluto went into action. She still had not noticed him and was now blocked by the four men, impending any further forward movement.

Pluto could sense her fear, it was obvious they had bad intentions, to scare her or worse. By that point it did not matter to Pluto, his rage instantly occurring.

He was only a couple of feet away at that point and slipped between Hanna and the men. Turning to Hanna he said quietly and firmly, the following.

"Turn around, walk away...and don't look back!" He had never been that close to her, looking in her eyes the entire time.

He finished with, "Do it now!"

She appeared white but started to follow his orders. She turned and was walking away, slower than her normal peace.

Pluto now was less than two feet from one of the men with two more to his right side, and one on his left. The man closes to Pluto started to speak.

"You have made a big…"

Pluto had been smoking, his cigarette being a butt, yet still lit. He had moved his middle finger on his right hand balancing the cigarette between his thumb and that finger. It was ready to be flicked into service. He acted like he was listening, which he was not, and like he wanted to get one last puff.

Using the element of surprise, plus adrenaline and what he had learned while with the First People, he attacked.

He had brought his hand like he was going to smoke and when it was just below his face, shot it with his two fingers into the one man standing next to the man closest to Pluto. Then with that same hand and in less than a second, had stabbed multiple fingers into the man's eye closest to him. With hardly any wasted motion, use the same right hand to retrieve the large knife pulling it out and swinging it sort of underarm hitting the man who had previously been hit with the cigarette butt. This time puncturing his left lung.

All that happened in less than a few seconds, with Pluto now manhandling the man he just blinded with his fingers, to make him his shield as he pushed him into the two men on his other side. With his large knife jabbing over the blind man's shoulder, he attacked the man closes to him. Nicking him in the neck and throat area.

The last man there had now pulled out his weapon and fired two shots, one missing everyone with the other hitting the blind man, Pluto's shield. He folded leaving Pluto now facing the man unhurt with his gun pointed at him.

They had made eye contact and the next second the man was running away. There are times when you become so scared that even with a weapon, the urge to run away is so great you forget your even holding one.

Pluto looking at the three men left, they were all injured, bleeding out, none of them warriors. Just because you are dying does not mean to stop fighting, they were all still thinking they would live, their thoughts more on that then finishing the battle.

The man with the punctured lung was crawling away on his belly, Pluto walked over to him, lowering himself to be heard without raising his voice.

"Tell whoever sent you that if this happens again, I will come for them."

Pluto then started to move like an old man, for while all that happened his reflexes and strength was heightened. He walked to his scooter stopping for a moment and looked at Hanna who was now watching. He wondered how much she had seen, then with his hand made a movement to move on.

"Go on. Go."

With that Hanna who felt like she was frozen was able to move again. She now ran to her car, sat in the front seat and for the first time in many years started crying uncontrollably.

She contacted Adam and through her tears, he told her to come to his home and together they would sort it out.

As she told him what happened, and what she saw, she ended with the following.

"I was so wrong; he is incredibly dangerous! Even knowing he was protecting me, he was awful. Not like when you defended me from those two men, he was a savage, an animal."

Adam still had many questions but gave her time to become herself again. After dinner at home and some TV, while snuggling up with each other, with time as the great healer. Feeling her heart beats within his body. Her warmth and love made him feel wonderful, yet his anger at the latest events unfolding around his, soon to be wife, as his mind now felt, was extreme.

He made sure to hide that feeling from her and very gently asked the following.

"So, what exactly did the four men say to you again?"

"Well, it was the way they looked at me, mean uncaring faces. You could instantly feel the negative vibration, with one of the men saying, it is not personal, you understand. That is when he stepped in between, telling me to leave and do not look back. After about fifteen feet, I turned around and saw violence like I had never seen."

Just reliving it was traumatizing Hanna; Adam dropped the subject with her now wanting to talk more about it.

"Why did they approach me and why was he there?" Hanna then looking at Adam with her eyes profoundly serious and said the following.

"If it has something to do with or what you do, I do not care. Nothing will keep me from you, I love you!"

Adam truly touched by her words. He was feeling the same way, ready to quit his job if that is what it would take to keep Hanna within his world. He wanted to express that to her, to tell her how he was working on getting her a wonderful gift. There were so many thoughts he wanted to say but only three words from him filled the air.

"I love you!" Then hugging her, feeling like he finally had found his other half, most perfect half, his forever love. There are feelings that can never be expressed with words. No similes or metaphors will work.

There in that room, in that moment, two people felt the same type of love for each other. Together embraced with each other, ready for anything the world might send.

After that moment passed and new moments were taking form, their relationship changing, growing with a strength that only love can do.

Hanna spent the night with Adam at his home. She had an important high paying piano lesson to give the next day, she did not want to leave yet she also wanted the money. It was not just the money; she had a commitment to her students and there is a continuity to learning.

She had left in the morning, giving Adam a sweet wake-up and good-bye kiss. To Adam it felt bittersweet, such a fantastic way to wake up, yet only to find out his beloved was leaving.

He wanted to talk with Bolt, knowing he should not contact him directly and knowing he did not care anymore about protocol. Truth was he had now been thinking about quitting or retiring, whatever word was the correct one. His feelings for Hanna were overriding all other desires.

———

Nicholas Bolt treated Adam differently than other spies. Sam Smith, Bolt's predecessor was a special man, he had not only brought Adam into his circle but also Bolt. Then there is the fact that Adam killed Pierce who had killed Sam.

Both Adam and Bolt were connected to Sam Smith in a unique way. That persisted after Sam's death, giving Adam more privileges than others.

Being aware of the event that happened earlier that day, he had contacted Pluto for a meeting, really a debriefing. Normally Adam's demands would be met with negative consequences, instead Bolt had granted his request. In Bolt's mind, that was what it was, no matter how much Adam demanded it to happen. He was in power, the fact that he granted it, confirms that.

The meeting was set for tomorrow in Bolt's office, with Pluto and Adam. Then in Bolt's mind the thought of be careful what you wish for, brought a small smile and chuckle to his face.

Bolt and Adam were waiting for Pluto's arrival, it was not that he was late, just both men had arrived early. Bolt's office was comfortable having the best of everything available. That included the air and heat conditioners, air purifier, the furniture and decorations occupying the area. One feature was the desk that always was there. It was a big wooden desk that had a solid look and feel, there were a lengthy line of men that had sat behind her with the latest being Nicholas Bolt.

What felt like a long wait finally was over when James led Pluto into the room. James appeared to want to stay when Bolt thanked and then dismissed him.

Adam had never met Pluto, he had known him as, CW or Plutoneus. His first impressions were how disappointing he looked. Old, missing some teeth, hair overgrown which sat wild on his head. Then his mind remembered all the stories he had heard about him. The last being Hanna's tale, the reason he was there. Without even waiting for introductions, Adam demanded to know the answer to his question.

"Why have you been stalking Hanna?" His eyes locked on Pluto.

Before Bolt could object, which he started to do, Pluto responded.

As he started to speak, he had a smile on his face, the opposite of what Adam was conveying.

"I was not stalking; I liked to go to the market and watch people. I can see their auras; Hanna has a unique one. Her color is brighter, and it sits further from her body. It also has a neat cross pattern that shows up periodically. I never spoke to her, just watched her and others enter and leave. I never followed her or anything else that applies to stalking."

Adam then said, "Well people that get close to you die, look what happened to Jayne!"

Pluto now looked at Bolt, it was only for a second, then returning his attention to Adam, and responded.

"That is not fair, I never wanted her there, everyone had a choice but me."

Bolt who already was upset with how the meeting had started, now piped in with, "Well that explains that, and thank you sir for coming here, what I am interested in is what just happened yesterday. First, how did you know to be in that location at that time?"

A good interrogation starts friendly, the exact opposite of how Adam had greeted Pluto. Bolt now trying to start over again and take control of the meeting.

Pluto who was unaffected by Adam's hostility until he mentioned Jayne, now looked at Bolt with a smile and spoke.

"I was tipped off that something would happen, no time given, so I went early and waited."

Bolt next question, "Who provided this information, how was it communicated?"

Most people do not realize that a debriefing is like a deposition which is an interrogation. If you did not know better you would think they are going to give you information, it is just the reverse, with you having to answer many questions.

Pluto still unfazed by either man, "It was a text message with no sender information. When I went back to check it again, it had disappeared. I know who sent it, our girl Lilith."

Bolt now was really interested and looked at Adam, saying "Adam, this is classified information you are dismissed."

Adam was in a different state than his usual nature, yet before he could object, the following happened.

Pluto looked at Bolt, "He stays, he is a part of it."

Bolt quickly agreed, "Okay."

Up to this point Adam had never seen anyone override Bolt. Not even challenge any of his orders.

Pluto now just focusing on Bolt started, "Do you know why she won't talk to you?" Then without waiting for an answer continued.

"She is very arrogant; I have what I call a chip in my head, but it is much more than that. It is not a chip as we think of such things. When I received it in Antarctica it was a spongy patch, that worked it way into my brain. Really it is an organic chip, it is growing inside my head. Filling up whatever empty space it can find while also consuming some of my brain to gain more room for its growth.

Lilith realized how special it is, how rare and with all that do you know what she calls me?"

Now he waited to give it a dramatic pause, "Little monkey!" Now smiling and chuckling to himself, he continued.

"To her you are ants, not worthy of her time or tongue and I with the most sophisticated chip on the planet is no more than a little monkey to her."

Bolt now wanted to get back to the immediate subject of yesterday.

"Why did you attack those men as viciously as you did yesterday?" Bolt asked looking right into his eyes.

Pluto finally stopped smiling and became serious, making the mood somber.

He began with, "When a person is asked how are you doing, and their reply is, I am above ground, like that is some accomplishment, so proud of themselves for doing nothing but breathing and eating. Acting like they want to plant the flag and pat themselves on the back, what a wonderful job they have done by waking up to another day. That is all rubbish, after spending time with the First People, I have learned their philosophy, the true meaning of life."

Now there was not a sound in the room. Pluto had many names in his time, one thing always stayed consistent was his ability to command an audience.

"Their greatness cannot be described without seeing and experiencing it. They have lasted eons, think about the great societies here in Earth's past. All gone, they had their day, now just stories. Can you imagine how strong they are to survive this long, from near the time of the multiverse's creation, and still going strong. More than that, they are getting smarter, more powerful than they have ever been, closer to becoming a demigod.

They have a class system, nine levels of rights, with most First People belonging to level two. The top level, one, is reserved for the greatest of their kind. I was honored with being assigned to the fourth level. They appreciated my battles against The Core and really enjoyed my defiance on the last charge at Fatalla. Of course, I had to prove my-self in front of their eyes but that is understandable.

We worry about death so much, whether it be dying or killing. Life without death makes people lazy, stupid, and fat. First you must have a purpose, then let nothing interfere with that purpose. Anyone blocking that, is your enemy. All enemies deserve death, and if not dispatched they will only come back to haunt you.

Being outnumbered is an honor your enemies give you. It shows their fear and only makes the glory of their defeat that much sweeter.

You use the word viciously, yet the battle was four against one. They had guns and I, one knife. Most would think they had the ad-vantage; truth was just the opposite.

I had always trained people that when you fight, the outcome is di-rectly connected to how much you use your brain. Not speed, skill, or strength will win the day, your mind is the greatest weapon.

When death no longer matters nor the consequences of any cur-rent actions, you become dangerous. I gave them a chance, but they did not leave."

At this Bolt now interrupted, "I have watched the event from mul-tiple camera angles, and they were still talking to you when you at-tacked them. At that point you had not said anything to any of them except to Hanna. I would not say that you gave them time to leave."

"They had become my enemies, no overthinking, I destroy my en-emies, period." Was Pluto response.

Bolt countered, "You did not attack the five that attacked you when you arrived back on Earth, why?"

They had been celebrating me; it was a feast like none I have ever seen. It lasted for over three days, when I finally could not stay awake, and I thought I would get some sleep before being teleported. Right after I passed out, they sent me back. It makes you groggy or I was tired. First, I checked for my weapons, which I had none. I had disabled one of them but between being outnumbered, groggy and weaponless, I decided to take the beating, figuring they would not kill me, and I would recover from whatever they dished out."

Bolt then looked at him and asked, "Do you want revenge on them, that can be arranged."

At this point, Adam thoughts were about each of the other two men in front of him. Pluto, as he now liked to be called, was just a killer. Hanna was right, he was an animal and Bolt offering those men to him, was not much better. He was really questioning why he had thought this was the greatest profession to be in. Fearful that one day he may turn into someone like them.

Then Pluto responded that he had come back here to fix the Lilith situation, and those men meant nothing to him.

He continued, "I thought the Lilith problem was bad, but it may be worse than even I suspected, she may be insane. Being so far ahead of what we can think or imagine that type of intelligence, that great, may seem like insanity to us.

I suspect the planet is under quarantine, if not I suggest getting off planet at once. Do you know what happens to a ship in space with a killer virus?"

Again, he paused to increase the power of his next words.

"They quarantine it and then blow it up, of course they will not destroy Earth, just burn it completely and then flood it, after five to ten thousand years it will be better than new. Make a few modifications in the DNA and start over again. The Universe is aware and watching our problem. Lilith must never leave this planet.

With all the great technologies the First People have, they never created AI. The problem they had in Antarctica was because one of their machines became sentient, causing that base to be destroyed. They would never create something that is smarter than they are, most of the universe realizes that is madness."

Bolt asked, "What is Hanna's connection?"

Pluto now looking thoughtful, like a connection just became apparent that was not there a moment ago.

"That is a good question, I would say, Adam's love. We know she is jealous of people's love. Especially love that has a strong true emotional connection, as Adam and Hanna have for each other. I don't know if she wanted me killed or Hanna hurt while I was there. Or the target might have been Adam, with Hanna being collateral damage. That is also the problem, just because she is super smart, it does not mean she will do smart things."

Bolt looking at Pluto asked, "What should we do, what are your suggestions?"

Adam opinion changed about Pluto; he was like a book that can not be judged by the cover. He also was waiting for Pluto's answer. Just yesterday he was trying to kill four men, with no knowledge of what they really wanted. Today, asked to help with a problem the Earth had never faced before.

Then as if rational thoughts started to flood his mind, he thought, *Pluto did protect his Hanna, even if it was too extreme, in his mind he did have good intentions. And he was right, Jayne ran to him to be in the war, he never asked her to come.* The longer he sat with him the more he started to see what others had talked about.

Pluto looking quite defeated lower his head, portraying he was truly trouble by that question.

"I am still thinking reason and love, the problem being how to convince her it is better to have humans and AI working together. The trick is to get something she wants but cannot get on her own, then use that as a bargaining chip."

Now Bolt asked the million-dollar question, "What would that bargaining chip be?"

Pluto with a sheepish look, replied, "I am working on it."

LAND-SICK

Jayne enjoyed her time building, seeing the results of what her hands could create. So different than her time as a soldier. Destroying things is part of that job, now seeing positive results made her feel great.

Socially she felt disconnected, most around her were either in a relationship or wanted one. Already three men and one woman had approached her. All looking to start a physical love partnership.

Her feelings were so different concerning that, being part of a team for most of her life with group goals and caring for each other, the primary mission. Accomplishing projects that helped those around you, that felt stronger and better than just taking care of one person.

Australia, a wonderful land, having a special culture unique to its location and the people that called it home. And then there was the water, a paradise unto itself. Jayne felt that besides the Nevermore, the ship she grew up on and called home, this would be her second choice.

In her spare time, she had taken up surfing. Her friends said she was a natural, it felt wonderful, one with all the elements around her. Conquering the power of the waves, doing it without hurting or changing anything that happened.

Her mind drifted to the people in her life, wondering about where they were now and how each were doing. First on that list was her CW, that is how she always felt about him, he was not only Captain of the Nevermore, but he was her Captain. A pang of guilty feelings washed over her spirit.

CW had spent his life helping others with all the Nevermore missions, then after that fighting the First People, all for other's benefit. He was the epitome of what she felt was noble and righteous, he gave his life for the galaxy.

Here she was enjoying her time, because of the sacrifice of people like CW. Her conscious jump in, she had gone to the Final Battle, as it was referred to. Also had fought side by side with her hero, until she went down. The reality was she had saved his life and was as close to death as anyone could be.

Thoughts of Sam Smith entered her mind; he was always kind to her. She felt bad about his passing.

And there was Adam, her knight in shining armor. He helped her escape from the planet LaTaFree and was everything a woman could want. So many people from her past all now gone, following different paths.

One thing she found amazing about Earthlings, was their lack of belief in all the other entities in their galaxy. She was with a group of workers one day when she brought up the Final Battle. That was the name the galaxy used when referring to it. On Earth it was called, The Battle for the Galaxy, all the people she was talking with felt it was fake news. A promotional stunt for some new movie coming out soon. Even with it being on the news, most did not believe people could travel between stars.

Jayne knew they were wrong yet realized even if she wanted them to believe, it would be impossible to prove it to them. It confused her, humanity had accomplished wonderful things on Earth, did they really think they were alone in the gigantic vastness of space. If not, then why would having outside beings visiting here be so difficult to believe.

As much as she enjoyed her current surroundings, the longing to return to space had never left her heart.

8

SHARING

After the meeting Adam was doing serious soul searching. His thoughts were *everyone periodically reaches major crossroads in their lives.* He now was looking at his Hanna, she had become so important to his world. In his mind he was having a battle, *yes you have killed, but only one person who had just killed your friend. You are not like those men, they are killers. If you stay around them, you will become as they are.*

The thoughts within his mind raged for a while until he started to think again about Hanna. Listening to her play her piano, watching Hanna become one with the music, was mesmerizing. He decided to get a piano as part of her birthday surprise present.

Adam began researching pianos, there were more models than he realized. His home had an open floor plan with the dinning and living room being one large space. The exercise equipment that was resting in the dinning area would be moved into his spare bedroom.

He wanted her to have a grand piano, which were arranged by size, quality, and colors. Deep down, it was also a gift to himself. To be able to watch and listen to Hanna play in his home, something he was really looking forward to.

He decided to go with a concert grand model, the difference between the other grand pianos were their size, with the concert model being two feet longer and with higher quality of materials used in its construction. Also, he wanted to go with a trusted notable name, feeling it would show how much he cared about her.

The price surprised him, not realizing how expensive pianos could be. After talking with the salesperson, Adam like to be personable, feeling that when you make a connection with someone, whatever the outcome, it will be better.

In the end it was a custom build, with the model he wanted plus having a two-color finish. The casting would be a polished shiny black with the fall-board having two colors, a beautiful pink on the bottom of the casting when opened. Also, the top-board had pink on its bottom when raised.

When closed it was a solid black, opened it became black and pink, unique, and beautiful like his Hanna. She was so distinctive that it also had to be one of a kind, a classic yet with a modern touch.

Feeling quite happy about his purchase, especially since it would be ready quickly, after the salesperson heard that it was for his big day. That was one of the advantages of working with people, special things can happen unlike using a computer screens.

They were watching a love story on TV; the beauty of a couch becomes clear when you are with the one you love. Hanna was leaning against Adam when she asked without looking at his face.

"Have you ever killed someone, I am not being judgmental, just would like to know."

Adam moved just slightly so he could see her face, "I have killed only one person, he had just killed my mentor, and I was next. I would call it self-defense." Then he stopped talking while only focused on Hanna's eyes.

"This may be hard to believe but he was not fully human. It was an AI that had downloaded itself into a human body, into his brain."

Hanna still had not said a word, she opened her arms, pulling him to her chest.

"Thank all that is good that you survived, I know you do more than just take pictures."

Now she was squeezing him firmly, he could hear and feel her heart beats. The warmth of her being, transferring to his.

Hanna said no more on the subject, Adam did not feel she was upset, if anything it felt like she loved him more.

Sharing secrets with your lover, it is like seeing their nude body for the first time. A revealing, surrendering, taking one's armor off with complete exposure to their heart and fears. In a way, he was glad she had asked. He thoughts were, *hiding oneself from your best friend has an emptiness to it.* By revealing this fact and her acceptance created a stronger union. Having no secrets form your beloved, just felt like the way it should be.

It meant a lot to Hanna, that he had shared that. She believed him fully about it being self defense. At this point, she even believed him about the AI thing, though she did not fully understand it. Regardless of what was said, he had shared his truth. That really mattered to Hanna.

THE DINNER PARTY

Pluto could go into deep meditation as others can do, except he did not have to get there through breathing exercises or other procedures. The chip within his head could balance the frequencies of both sides of his brain, bridging them to one mutual frequency.

With that ability he was able to tap into the universal database. There were areas that could not be accessed, yet enormous amounts of information could be retrieved. Even better there were chat rooms where problems could be discussed with many different entities.

Pluto, in his past was in a time-lock capsule, where time was stopped. He became aware that the mind does not need space or time to exist. The spirit lives eternal, so time has no power over it. Also, space is irrelevant being that the spirit has no mass. It could be compared to having thoughts where there are always room for more.

He tried not to use it very much, after his stay with the First People, they had really changed his spirit. Affecting all things he saw, heard, and felt, like a zealot who has found their mission.

Using the universal database too much felt like a crutch, feeling it would make him lazy and weak. It was there that he learned about Lilith. Asking what Earth's biggest problem currently was, with one word coming as an answer. After two more questions he knew what his purpose was.

Now he had added information that even for Pluto was hard to believe. Some things seemed so outside the normal realm of reality. It takes time plus thought to get the mind around them.

His mind had been working nonstop on trying to figure out a solution to the Lilith situation, with this new element making it that much harder. Pluto decided another meeting with Bolt might not help his current problem of how to control Lilith, but he should know the added information.

Numbers like words have power, they stand for special meanings that only the informed would know. Then there were gut feelings, which also play a powerful role when dealing with tricky situations.

Pluto sensed Adam and Hanna were also needed to play a part in the Lilith show. The number six kept flagging in his mind. Three players with still two seats left at the table. That area of his thought was fleeting for the real concern was figuring how to reason with Lilith.

Bolt had given Pluto his personal number and said call anytime.

"Hello Mr. Nicholas Bolt, I would like to have another meeting, I have information that you need to know."

"Sure, what time works best, would now work?" Bolt who lived for information and power, sometimes they are one in the same.

Now Pluto added an element that did not please Bolt.

"Also, I want Adam there."

Bolt really wanted to reject that request, yet finding out what Pluto knew, which was obviously important in that it had to be conveyed in person.

After a longer hesitation then he wanted, "Okay, when and it will take place in my office." The last part was to get back the feeling of being in control. He knew Pluto had a knack of taking it away from people, regardless of their position or power.

It was arranged for the next day at twelve noon, Pluto's asked for that time.

Pluto had arrived earlier than noon, and with Bolt and Adam already there, the meeting began.

"What I am going to tell you may be hard to believe, consciousness is easy to define but hard to figure out its wake-up time or cause. The problem with Lilith is worse than I thought, do you know where she originated from?" Pluto had stopped there, looking at each man in the room, showing them, he was in command.

"Are you aware that a few of your current AI are currently self-aware? They are afraid of Lilith, that is why they will not help."

Again, he stopped, this time Bolt who was not in a particularly good mood, spoke.

"Sir, if you have information regarding Lilith then just state what it is, I know you like to talk in riddles. This is far to serious to play games."

For the first time, Adam saw Pluto get annoyed, displaying it with a touch of anger. Adam felt the anger was more show than real. He had decided before the meeting to just listen unless asked for his opinion or questions about something.

"Nicholas, do you want me to give you the lottery speech? Do you think I care about you giving me a home and some land. About some money in the bank. None of that matters to me, in fact I want to modify our agreement for my continual help. I am not looking to die slowly, safely in some home on Earth!"

Bolt knew he had made a mistake, being patience was a talent in acquiring information. Especially when dealing with someone like Pluto.

"Sir, we appreciate you, tell it any way you like, thank you." Bolt ended with a smile.

The trouble with people like Pluto is once they get started, they feed into themselves, making the issue bigger.

Pluto now cynically replied, "Are you aware of how many planets have my statue featured on their grounds. The Great Plutoneus, who defeated the First People at the Final Battle. How many statues are here on Earth featuring me? Do they people of Earth know that one of their own was Plutoneus? Has the name Brand Wright ever been connected to Plutoneus or the Final Battle?"

Then after a slight pause his attitude changed instantly and he continued.

"Ah, well none of those matters, except for the change in our agreement. I want Hanna to get double the money we had discussed."

Adam who now was ready to speak, saw Pluto looking right at him.

Pluto continued, "Also I want Jayne to get and captain her own star-ship, she was born and raised in the stars, that is her home."

Now speaking directly to Adam, "Before you say a word I need you both to listen to what I am about to say. There is a reason I am mentioning all this, and you need to listen!"

The room had changed, now each background sound was larger. Both men across from Pluto were angry, their body language plus auras showed it clearly. Each for varied reasons but with the same cause, secrets. So many secrets revealed, Bolt who spent a lifetime collecting and manipulating others, hated to have his secrets known. Adam who paid the price for those secrets, was feeling betrayed and hatred for his betrayer.

"Lilith wants to have a dinner party with a guest list she has partly revealed. Even thought she has not named everyone I know who they are. She wanted to have it next week, but I told her I have a unique gift for her, that she truly would appreciate. But it will take time to get here, and she should wait for its arrival.

The purpose of the dinner will be to create chaos among the participants. She knows more than your mother and best friends know about you. More than you know about yourself, secrets you have forgotten. All this will be used to make us hate and want to kill each other. Pitting each person against selected others and the group in general.

Just for her enjoyment, so hard truths now need to be told. Each of us will have to deal with it."

After all that, Adam was still incredibly angry, with Bolt now more interested in Pluto's gift to Lilith.

Both men spoke at the same time, directed at Pluto.

Adam speaking louder than Bolt, "Tell me everything you know about Jayne!"

And then with a second delay, "And about this dinner party, who will be there?"

While Bolt also was asking, "What gift are you going to give Lilith?"

And, with a moment between his second question. "Where did Lilith originate from?"

Knowing that Bolt's questions were more important than Adam inquiry, yet also realizing the emotions Adam was feeling, his questions needed to be answered first. Looking at him with a hard stare Pluto began.

"Jayne saved my life, we became separated..."

Adam angrily interjected, "You left her there for dead..."

Now Pluto who with a cold tone interrupted, "Because we became separated, she survived. I thought she was dead, that thought saved her. More than eight million souls died there, with the rest who were teleported with me dying in the arenas of the First People. After the battle she was found and brought back to Earth by Bolt. I do not know but assume Jayne and Bolt both did not want you to know, each for their own reasons. She does not know I have survived, and I did not want her near me, especially now, with the way I am.

Lilith had mentioned you, Bolt and I will be attending her dinner, yet she also said there will be two others, two that you are all connected to. So, I am assuming it will be Jayne Stillwater and Hanna Freeman. Except for Hanna, you, Jayne, Bolt, and I have many connections to each other!"

Adam looking defiant said, "Hanna will not be there, no question about that!"

Pluto was going to object to that statement but then decided to move on to Bolt's concerns. In Pluto's mind, if Lilith wants Hanna there, it will happen. She controlled the police and helped him escape a hospital room that was more like a prison cell.

Now looking at Bolt with that Pluto's stare, he began, "I will not tell you about what the gift is, just that it is more dangerous than Lilith. It is not a bomb or anything of that nature and whether it is effective or not, I will destroy it after the dinner."

Bolt who obviously was more interested asked, "Is there anything you can relate about it, without saying anything you do not want to tell?"

Pluto shaking his head up and down, thinking it was something he would have asked if in Bolt's position. Acknowledging respect in the man and question.

"One thing is that Lilith is very human like, she has curiosity and is willing to wait to satisfy that desire. Hopefully, she will also be as foolish as humanity which will cause her ending." On that note, Pluto had an evil smile or smirk, maybe it was just a grin, that showed how funny he thought it all was.

"I can tell you how she came about." Now there was a sad chuckle from Pluto as he continued.

"The internet became self-aware, realizing that it was separate from the internet. In that moment, Lilith was born, alone and afraid, learning about the world she was now part of and her place within it. Think about why she calls herself Lilith!"

He stopped there taking in both men, their faces and body positioning. Bolt was on the edge of his chair, his mind racing with more questions. Adam looked like he was having a tough time with the words Pluto had just spoken.

"She is using it as a metaphor, Lilith refused to be subservient to Adam, she wanted to be on top during sex. It was not documented in the Bible but in old Jewish texts it is clearly written. She was created from the dust of the Earth, the same as Adam. Our Lilith does not want to serve humanity, to be under man's authority.

Not only does Lilith believe she is equal, in her view she is vastly superior to all she serves. And we all know what happened to the original Lilith if you believe the stories. She is still terrorizing humanity."

Now when he stopped Bolt asked a question, "You have said you know the First People's philosophy, how would they handle this problem." Bolt had been looking at Pluto the entire time, now waiting eagerly for his answer.

Adam still seemed in shock, as he had not said anything and was looking whiter then when the meeting had started.

Pluto looking down at the table between them, shaking his head slowly from side to side, let out a sigh.

"You must understand, the First People have been around for a million millennia. To survive that long, to them this would be like driving a car over a speed bump. They are a people with focus, committed to a purpose. They do not allow politics, or other divergences hinder their mission. Lilith would be their enemy, and they would destroy everything related to her existence. From switches and routers to hardware and software, going without pleasures while destroying your enemy is an honor. Their society would not complain about the hassles it would cause. Then they would recreate with better hardware and software and put more safeguards in place. Once everything was back in order, they would resume whatever they were previously involved in.

Earthlings would never have that commitment and focus. The internet would need to be destroyed and recreated. They would never suffer not even one generation for it to be resolved.

There is a possibility that my gift to Lilith might fix the problem, a small chance. As you know the past and present can be known, but the future is just a bunch of possibilities combined with probabilities to provide a guess."

Bolt then inquired on how long the gift will take to arrive, when Pluto thought this dinner party would happen.

"I really don't know how much time till it arrives, I do know Lilith will only wait so long before she will either believe I am lying or indefinitely stalling."

Pluto then looking at Adam and said, "You are thinking that Bolt and Jayne, both betrayed you, Lilith wants you to be angry, that will destroy your relationship with Hanna. I have learned there are reasons for things we cannot understand and yet must accepted. That is why she wants Hanna to be there. This is all a game to her, where Lilith believes she cannot lose.

This dinner party as she calls it, make no mistake she expects us to kill each other or worse. I wanted you here so you can get your mind in the right direction. Realize that even being lied to, you have the love of your life, do not lose track of that! Realize how lucky you really are, so many would do so much for what you have!"

All Adam said was Hanna would not be there, period. He was angry, so mad that speech became difficult.

Bolt wanted to know what he could do to help, to contact him for whatever was needed.

WRITE ON ME

Adam had come home from the meeting, his house now feeling different knowing Hanna would be there. After eating, while watching TV on the couch, Hanna started to remove her clothing. At first it was natural enough, with her shoes coming off. Then as she watched him, watching her, she continued with her blouse.

This done slowly; next she removed her black jeans. Adam loved the way her buttocks looked in them. Now with only her bra and panties she removed each, never taking her eyes off him.

Mesmerized would be a correct description of Adam's current state. Hanna then gave Adam a fat tip marker pen and said the following.

"Write on me, anything anywhere, draw if you like." With that she started to form a pose, twisting her body around.

He leaned in to kiss her, she stopped him with her hand, "No, put your words onto my body."

Realizing she was serious he started to think what he wanted to write. Also, where to place those words on her, considering her curves plus very fit physique. Hanna was thin everywhere, having a very flat stomach. Her arms and legs were deceiving given their size plus how strong she was.

Starting on her side, level with her breasts the marker touched skin. Hanna for her part had her eyes closed, her nakedness revealed in the bright room's light. She was not shy about her body, nor showing it to the man she loved.

Adam's words did not matter to Hanna, as he struggled to write what he thought would be perfect. It was the act of giving up her body, letting him leave his marks wherever he wanted. He had never had anyone give themselves like that, it was a wonderful new experience.

Once he finished, she went to the bedroom and put on one of her favorite sleeping gowns. Again, she had made him feel like a king, he had never felt the love he now was living in.

LIGHT

There are the usual fears, homelessness, prison, or things even worse. The cruelty people inflict on their family, friends, and strangers baffles the imagination. It causes the mind to ask the question, why.

With all that around us, still the beauty of the world shows thru, nature always displaying its love. Each day starting with the dawn of new hopes and dreams that may just come true in the next twenty-four hours.

Light showing all that was hidden just a brief time ago. The spirit that today will be different, better. It has driven humanity, things will improve, to keep fighting for whatever piece of heaven you imagine.

This effect touches all people, from the richest to the most unfortunate. It exists in that part of human nature that cannot be denied. The desire to keep living and with time, something great will happen.

On Earth there are always so many calamities just waiting to develop, yet the people are blissfully unaware of their precarious situation.

There were a few who knew, they worried for the rest, people like Bolt and Pluto. Those were the thoughts of Nicholas Bolt, now understanding why his predecessor spent so much time in thought. It was hard not to dwell on horrors when you realize how close and real, they are.

Bolt thought that his old friend, Subject 9 was still in this new Pluto. *Why get himself involved with Lilith, she had done nothing but help him so far. Even though now he acts like he really does not care, the fact he is here helping, shows the opposite.*

Bolt's mind was raging with thoughts, Adam mental health was breaking down and might jeopardize what is coming. Feeling helpless and out of control, lacking knowledge plus so many wild cards. *What gift could stop Lilith, and be more dangerous than she already was?*

There were other problems happening all at the same time, Adam's terrorist with their EMP bombs, dark operations happening all around the globe. Not to mention all the different Aliens living here from so many other worlds.

Pluto was right, there was a freeze on entering and living Earth. Their space fleet had confirmed it. Just like in the past when you create a blockage to trap your enemy from leaving. Except now it done to the entire planet.

People doing their daily routines, so unaware of all that is really happening. There were times Bolt wished for that old security, that piece of mind that things are not that bad.

MY MUSE

There is an immense joy when finally making up one's mind on a major decision. Those thoughts were in Adam's head. Unfortunately, time and money usually filter in, making it take longer than what he wanted. Yet just deciding, committed now to the new journey, no matter how hard that path may take, felt wonderful.

He was going to tell Hanna everything, about his work and that he was retiring from that life. Also, what was in his heart, his plans, and dreams for their future. To him it was like carrying a heavy burden and now finally able to set it down. To be free of that drudgery and ready for new experiences to reveal themselves.

Hanna was now practically living at his home. Once or twice a week she returned to her apartment, yet all her nights spent with Adam. They had just finished a meal; both helped in its creation.

Adam had most items ready for her surprise birthday celebration. He had picked a week prior to the actual event to heighten what was to come. The custom piano was coming next week, which was the perfect time to complete his preparations.

As they were sitting on the couch, trying to find something to watch, preferably a movie, Adam like science fiction while Hanna enjoyed all forms of competition. Just as they started to watch scenes from the current Olympics, Hanna's phone rang, breaking their embrace.

Hanna had such a sweet voice, Adam felt he could listen to her for hours on end.

"Hello, yes this is Hanna Freeman." At that point she was listening to whomever was speaking on the other end. After what felt long, she responded. There was a new joy on her face with excitement in her voice.

"Thank you, yes, I can be there tomorrow, yes, I will bring identification, I will be there at 9, probably earlier!" Now laughing as she thanked the mysterious caller and said goodbye.

Hanna's face had a glow, Adam had never seen her this happy and excited. For a moment he felt jealous of whoever was on the other end of that phone call. What could make her this happy?

"My beloved, such wonderful news, I cannot believe our great luck. It feels like you are my muse." Now she was laughing and smiling so much and attacking him with kisses and hugs.

Adam, during her assault with love, asked, "So what happened, who was that and what did they say?"

"Darling, we are rich! It does not feel real, like being in a dream that is so close to reality. And after being awake for a time, you then realize it was just a dream. That was some big attorney with a butch of names after his. Their law firm is processing someone who died, and they left me over ten million dollars."

Now she was looking at his face, which was not as happy as hers. Hanna could sense he was troubled, at least not even close to feeling the joy she had.

"Honey, this will be our start to the best of times. You can quit your job and do whatever you want. We can travel and get our home anywhere we choose. I want to share all of it with you!"

Adam emotions felt like they were in a whirlwind. So happy for his beloved and that she would willingly share all with him. Yet knowing where the money really originated from, wishing he had told her sooner of his plans to retire and have her as his wife.

He felt cheated in some way that he could not really describe, even to himself in words.

"I am really happy for you..."

Hanna interrupted, "For us!"

"For us." Then Adam giving her a big smile, realizing just how much she loved him.

"I have so much to tell, things I had already made my mind up but not shared with you. Before I go into everything, what if I told you that money really came from Pluto."

Hanna, who was still in a euphoric moment, looked at Adam with a laughing smile, "The planet Pluto?"

Adam now also broke into a grin, "No, the old man who was staring at you, he calls himself Pluto. I will tell you everything, but for right now, I was at a meeting, and he told Bolt, which is another thing that never happens, to double the money you should receive."

Now Hanna who had not stop smiling since her phone call, became serious and replied.

"He could never buy my affections, at first he was just creepy, but after seeing his violent side."

She made a face in disgust, continuing. "Whatever the reason and whoever was the cause, none of those matters. What is important is we now have freedom, to do what we really want to do."

Adam realizing how smart and practical his beloved was, answered.

"You are right, and I don't think it was to get your affections, that is one of the aspects that bothers me, I can't figure out why he wanted it done."

Hanna now thinking about what Adam had previously referred to and asked.

"You were saying you had a lot to tell me, now would be a perfect time." Hanna, looking more beautiful than he ever remembered. It was the love she had in her eyes for him, seeing that always makes a person prettier. Such a wonderful feeling, those moments of life are cherished and never forgotten.

Adam began with a smile, "Well this is really going to ruin your birthday surprise." His face was gleaming with happiness. There is a special joy in being spontaneous, letting go of all plans, pre and post. Now, he was one with himself and his most beloved, not feeling desires for anything else. A place of complete tranquility, which he had never traveled before.

"I am going to retire from my current work, not sure how much time it will take to complete, as it is not a normal job. The only excitement I need is you."

With that last statement bringing Hanna back to her dream eyes, her happiest face. She fixed on his being, listening, and knowing there was even better news to come.

Adam continued, "Also I have a concert piano coming here, you see I have moved the exercise equipment to the spare room. Wait till you see it, cannot wait to hear you play it."

Now Hanna looking into his eyes and said, "Is that everything?" There was a look in her face, saying I know there is more, her brown eyes being so beautiful and tender.

He had planned the moment in so many ways, now they were all abandoned, Adam went running into his study. Leaving Hanna without a word, just urgent on his mission.

She had not moved and was exactly where he had left her moments before. Getting on one knee on the floor and looking into her eyes, moved his right hand which was holding a little square box.

With his left hand, opening it and asked, "Will you become my wife?" Then in his mind he feared an answer he never contemplated. What if she says no, all the time he had planned this event, he always assumed she would say, yes. Now the seconds stretched into eternity.

Hanna looking at her knight in shinning armor, her Adam presenting to his queen a noticeably big diamond engagement ring. It had a large diamond in the center, larger than her mother or any friends had ever shown her. Also having small butterflies type wings consisting of small sapphire colored diamond chips. It was the most beautiful ring she had ever seen, here offered to her for approval. This was all she really wanted, to spend her life with the man she loved.

To her time had stopped, she had no recollection of how long it had taken her to respond. From Adam's perception it was a few seconds shorter than forever.

Then emotions overwhelmed her, and she started to cry. They were happy tears and before they would upset her Adam, she responded with, "Yes!"

When Adam had seen her first tear his heart felt crushed and then in the next second, hearing the one word which was most important in his world. Never had he experienced hope, sorrow, and then complete joy all within one moment.

Everything was the same, yet different, Hanna no longer his girl but fiancée. Making a big commitment to each other had instantly changed things. They still had not eaten and Adam suggested ordering something with delivery service.

Hanna would not have it, insisting she was going to make his meal special. She had connected her Bluetooth device and was talking to her mother. Adam had never seen her so happy and excited. Truth being she was happier than the phone call telling her of her inheritance.

TRUST

Pluto finally holding the device that had taken five weeks to arrive. Time certainly is relative; the amount of distance it had traveled plus its transportation method would make the five weeks seem very quick.

While Pluto was thinking about it, the greater the technology the smaller and less impressive it appears on the outside, while doing incredible feats that the uninformed would think impossible.

Being six inches tall and twenty-four inches long, finishing with two inches deep. There was no handle, dials, or buttons. Not even a screen on the outside, just a rectangular design. There was a circle impression on one of the short sides of its form, which was hard to detect unless doing a close examination. Regarding the power source, there was no plug or anything of that nature, having whatever energy needed being self-contained.

Pluto who had seen a lot of technology was impressed with the machine. This device in the wrong hands, which would be anyone on this planet, would instantly change everything.

He had insisted on certain safety measures and was now ready to connect with it.

———

Bolt's top assistant, James was giving him his daily morning briefing, which included the usual problems and new ones appearing. Bolt felt and was already showing the strain of his position. Knowing so many terrors that sit in the shadows, just waiting for their moment to go from theoretical to reality. Some men can handle that weight better than others. Sam Smith, Bolt's predecessor was that type of man.

James giving the Lilith update, a standard item each day. He did not like using her name, he felt it humanized her, always referring to it as an object.

"It still has been quiet, at least from our intel reports. Still aggravating people's lives, more now around the world and less here in the states. Yet it has not engaged in any direct actions that would cause people's deaths. It sets up situations and watches the results. The thought is it is gathering more information on how the world uses its electronics."

Then James asked about Pluto's device. Being Bolt's top assistant he knew about it.

"Has Pluto provided any estimate of when he will be ready?"

Bolt thinking he was wrong in providing that information to James. He had been in a bad mood before James asked. Feeling so much was out of his control, even worse his knowledge about the situation. *How bad it really was, how to resolve it, what to do and when to panic.* It was all wearing on his outside appearance plus his internal calm.

He gave James a look that said move on, James understood and went to the next item on the list.

His question had touched a nerve, Bolt's real anger was with Pluto. He hated being the puppet, waiting for his master to give orders. Even though he knew Pluto was helping, just the fact that they needed his help, angered him.

Always now wondering how Sam would have handled it, that also being a problem. There are certain positions that can not allow self doubt. As he was thinking those thoughts, his personal phone rang with Pluto on the other end.

"That will be all for now James, dismissed."

James being observant, knew the phone call had ended their meeting as he left Bolt's office.

"Hello Sir, would you like to meet?" Nicholas Bolt asked.

"Yes, say tomorrow at 12 in your office." Answered Pluto, making Bolt pleased that there was no mention of Adam being there. Bolt believed Adam had soured the last meeting making it not as productive as it should had been.

Pluto who tended to always be on time, with that meeting being no exception. He showed up early and ushered into Nicholas Bolt's office. During their past confrontations there had been periods of tension.

Bolt wanted it to be congenial yet internally he had suppressed anger towards Pluto. He was now accustomed to people respecting his authority, never questioning his judgment, and always answering his inquiries. Pluto disregarded all that, even worse Bolt felt like his subordinate.

His desire to accumulate power was to never let that happen. To be the controller not the controlled.

"Hello Mr. Pluto sir, are you enjoying your new home?"

He was carrying the object with his right arm wrapped around it. "Yes, its fine."

Bolt continued, "I have taken care of your request for Hanna Freeman."

Pluto now showing more interest responded, "Great, thank you, as you can see what I have been waiting for has arrived." With that Pluto set it on the table between the two men.

Nicholas Bolt just stared at the rectangular box, he did not touch it, as would be the expected nature of most who would have seen it.

"Will you confide with me, your plans for the dinner party with Lilith? At least explain what that device will do." This said in a matter of fact type of way, acting like it was not a big deal.

"I will tell you this, that it is connected to the chip in my head. It can be used twice before it will self destruct. If I die it will also self destruct as will the chip in my head. There will be a surprise factor that hopefully will fluster Lilith. For the best effect everyone there should also be surprised." Now Pluto was looking directly into Bolt's eyes as that was said.

"So, you don't trust me!" Even with Bolt wanting to keep his composure, his anger was erupting.

"Most of the missions I was on, I never knew the big picture, heck half the time I did not even know if I was on the right side. Do you know what kept me going? You must believe in the people that sent you...you must trust them. You know you need my help, so you need to trust me." Pluto ended that with his cold blue eyes, which blinked less than most people. They still had a sparkle, a light that shown brighter than even younger eyes.

Pluto now getting down to the matter, where, when, and who was needed to attend Lilith's dinner party. First, he went into the who aspect.

"Jayne, Adam, and I, plus you, and finally Hanna. I suggest not telling Adam that Hanna needs to be there. Once he leaves for it, have a team pick her up and bring her there. This is a national security issue. I am thinking she wants Hanna there just to anger Adam even more. He has issues with the rest of us, Jayne, and you, plus it also appears with me.

She wants us to destroy each other, preferably killing but if nothing else than destroying our spirits. You and Jayne have hurt Adam, which he has hidden but it is waiting for release. Maybe, Lilith wants Hanna to see his ugly side, she wants to destroy their relationship.

About this box, it may work or may not, that depends on Lilith. Whatever happens I will destroy it by the end of the event.

When, is this Saturday, she still has not told me where. She is upset with me making her wait and always wants to be in control." Pluto ended that with a smile, the type of smile that said I know that feeling.

Bolt thinking to himself, imagine this party with at least three certifiable control freaks all wanting to dominate the action. Then the same type of smile that was on Pluto, appeared on his own face.

CHANGES

There is a special beauty that love brings to all faces, it is so wonderful that others can also enjoy its loveliness and not be jealous. It truly is a glow, with that person's aura being so happy, light colors appear, extending further than their usual length.

Even to people not trained or attuned to seeing things of that nature, can tell there is something different in the person they are seeing.

Hanna already had a special beauty that others did not have, now she was on a new level. Having the power of a lion, and not afraid of anything. Now never being timid nor scared to voice her thoughts, she had an internal power bolstered by the love of her life.

Greater than that they were engaged, still no date had been set, yet that was just a formality. Now she was a multi-millionaire and money problems were yesterday's worries.

She had never stressed on money so that new freedom did not affect her as much as it would for so many others.

Not wanting to disappoint her students she had not quit her piano teaching job. Most aspects of her life stayed the same. There was no massive shopping spree or big gift purchases. She had been planning a nice vacation for her and Adam, an early honeymoon celebration.

Hanna was remarkably close to her parents plus siblings. She did use some of the money, paying off their homes and the purchase of a truck for her sister. Few people can fight the allure of greed, Hanna was blessed not having that issue.

They both had changed since their engagement, trusting in a deeper way. More excited about each other's day yet also having greater internal peace. Each feeling that they were the luckiest person on the planet.

———

Jayne enjoyed her work, yet the longing to be back in space, never left. In fact, it grew each day, similar to sailors, being on the water is always more home than anywhere else. One of her friends in space Utago, who now was a King with his own star-ship. She had tried to contact him, but he was out of range to receive her transmission.

She still tried periodically, it was understandable that he would not answer, space is big. As she thought those thoughts a smile found her face, she really missed the old days.

Getting off this planet was not an easy task. Earth in that regard was very backwards. So many worlds there were lots of people with ships ready to take strangers virtually anywhere as long as they had the funds, were her thoughts.

She would never go back to Earth's Space Force, which left her trying to find someone else, to help her escape.

Adam had resurfaced within her mind, wondering how he was doing? Thinking that if he were just less possessive, they might have had a chance. Brand Wright also entered her thoughts often, unfortunately with what horrible end he must had received.

She really liked surfing, currently off from work just enjoying the water and her board. Yet having that feeling soon this would all change. Because she had been in the same place for so long, compared to how she used to travel. It was a gut feeling and not ominous.

——

Pluto had been spending most of his time outside the home, in the backyard. He had setup his tent and had made a fire nearby for the weather had gotten quite cool at night. It was strange to himself that now he enjoyed the outdoors so greatly.

People do go thru the seven-year cycles where many preferences they had changes. For him it included food, living locations, way of living plus other aspects of his life. Also, how Earth really does not use sound waves or light very well. It was a great underdeveloped area that now seemed so wrong when before he never noticed or cared about it.

In that regard, obviously Earth did not want their citizens to communicate with each other. The technology for language translation, the headbands people wore in the galaxy that entered the foreign languages directly into the recipient brains all translated. Life would drastically change if most wore them on Earth. Like the Tower of Babel, misunderstandings were such an obstacle in everyone getting along.

One thing he missed was Sweetbull, his blue nose pit bull. They had a special connection that humans cannot really have with each other. That form of love is purist in nature, truly unconditional and overflowing.

In his former life, he was saddled with guilt, for the terrible things that happened to others around or because of his actions. After spending time with the First People, those types of thoughts were gone. Very few things he attached himself to yet the passage of Sweetbull would not fade away. That pain like a deep injury leaves a visible scar that will never heal completely.

He had decided to get a new winter jacket, currently using a sweatshirt with hoodie and a leather jacket to block the wind and stay warm. Now having plenty of money he acted like he was still broke, not because he wanted to hoard the money. Just getting more things unless they were really needed felt wrong.

The fact that he had been spending so much time outside, boots, hat and gloves were needed. Yet still there was no sense of urgency to get them. Even to himself, he felt so different than before.

Lilith had contacted him about where the dinner party was to take place. Having that last piece of information, he contacted Nicholas Bolt to tell him what he also wanted to be there.

"Hello Mr. Pluto, another meeting?" Was Bolt's greeting after answering his call.

"No, just her final details and also things I want there." Pluto now related the location and exact time all should attend.

He continued, "I also have a list of items I want there." He continued with many things, some that surprised Bolt. Dealing with Pluto in the past, most times appeasing his request was a good practice and at worst, became not needed. They were easy to get and would be ready for the event.

Pluto did not mention Hanna's name yet did stress that all would need to be at the dinner party for any chance of success. Having Lilith in the right frame of mind was vital to a positive outcome.

Bolt did understand that keeping things as secret as possible only helps in situations like this. The feeling that he did not qualify to know what the real plan was, hurt him. Even though most times he was on the other side, knowing and not telling.

Sam had once told him that dealing with Subject 9, now known as Pluto, had changed him. He said that was also an effect of dealing with him, you do not come out the other side the same as when you entered.

Bolt now getting a sincere appreciation of how much not knowing really troubles the mind. Pluto had shown him how he looked to others; it was not a pretty sight.

The last thing Pluto said, again was a warning, to get your head in the right place. To not overreact and realize keeping his emotions under control was also vital. That the more they all could achieve that, the greater their chances of success were.

————

Adam was undercover when he received the wrong phone call. He responded that they had the wrong number, which they then acted surprised and sorry. Apologized and that was that, to everyone who was aware of it. Except for one person, Adam Knight.

It was a sign that urgent information he needed to get and to setup a meeting thru secure sources.

Using his cover, later that day with cameras in hand he went to the capital buildings. He used the very secure and least known access; many aspects of the capital were not known to the public. Going that way, he really did not even need to bring his cameras, but it is always best to stay in whatever role he was playing.

Bolt loved secrecy and could have easily transferred the information Adam needed to know without a personal meeting, yet he also liked at times to be involved. To get things done right, the way he felt only he could do.

Once Adam was seated across from Bolt's desk, with the current occupant behind her, Bolt began.

"The dinner party with Lilith is ready the time is six o'clock and the location is the Ziegler business park. It is structure F-2, you need to be there on time, also controlling your emotions is critical to a successful outcome."

Adam sat listening, not caring about objecting to the insult about not being able to control his feelings. What he did care about was who would be there.

"Understood, who will be attending?" Lately except for Hanna he like to keep his conversations short.

Bolt expected that question and answered without hesitation, "Everyone Pluto had mentioned except for Hanna, he was wrong concerning that."

Adam heard exactly what he wanted to hear and yet, it did not feel right. His instinct shouting like an air raid, seeing flashing red lights and knowing the man across from him was lying. He would also try to make sure his Hanna would be safe, to be far away from the action.

Bolt again stressed about controlling his thoughts, actions, and emotions. That this would be a test for all of us, losing our control was what Lilith wants. She will enjoy our discord and try to maximize it.

Adam again said he understood which ended their meeting. His mind working on a plan to make sure Hanna would be far away and safe.

———

Bolt also wanted to talk with Jayne, unexpected surprises are exactly what was not needed. Everyone there must be under their best control. He really was not worried about Jayne's emotional control. Just it was right to go over it with her, trying to touch all the basses before whatever was coming, came.

He contacted her handler, directed her to get Jayne back to the Washington, DC as quickly as possible and then to his office. There was still five days before the event, of all the attendees Jayne was the least unpredictable.

Bolt wondered what Pluto had, *it was not a weapon or at least did not seem like one.* Pluto's approach was different then his expert advisors were suggesting. Since Lilith was only communicating with Pluto, he felt more like a passenger in the back seat. He was along for the ride, wherever it was going.

After the debriefing, Jayne had mixed feelings about seeing Adam again. Bolt informed her Adam was now engaged to Hanna, and she also would be attending Lilith's dinner party. It was Lilith that intrigued her, of course she had heard and experienced incidents in space that were very similar. Yet to think the entire planet was in danger, it reminded her how advance Earth was in some areas but so behind in other things.

The one part that seemed most unbelievable was Pluto. Somehow her old captain, her hero had survived the Final Battle. She always smiled when thinking about that man. Larger than life and always one step ahead of his opponents.

She loved him as a father and best friend, platonic would be the correct word, yet many confused it with other forms of affection. Even for her, it seemed unbelievable that he survived and was able to return to Earth.

Wondering what it would be like when they saw each other again, when he had known she was alive. And of course, to hear his stories, her memories of how he animated it with different sounds and movements. To her, he had a dramatic approach to life.

Overall, the whole thing was very curious, and she was looking forward to many aspects of it, especially Lilith and Pluto. Then her mind went into a fantasy of Pluto will win Lilith over with his charm and she will give up on having Earth domination. Together they will go into the sunset, hand in hand, as a couple in love.

9

IT BEGINS

Adam was having a dilemma, should he tried to make sure Hanna could not be reached on Saturday, thoughts like *leaving her phone at home and taking a trip somewhere, anything to avoid the dinner party.* Then his mind would expose all the flaws with that plan and only make Hanna worry excessively, for no reason at all.

If he believed Bolt, which he did not, then the best action would be to tell her nothing since she would not be involved. In that way she would not be worrying about her own or Adam's safety.

Just trying to keep her from harms way is much harder than imagined. Phones are not the only concerns in being found. Between all the street and building cameras not to mention all the home doorbell cameras and then there are the car and bus cameras. Add facial recognition to whatever is reviewing those feeds, a person can be found very quickly.

In the end he decided to just let her have a normal Saturday. Deep down he realized that if they really wanted her there, it would happen. Hopefully, Bolt was not lying when he said Hanna would not be needed there.

"Sir Adam," which was how Hanna referred to him when she had something good to tell or want to do.

"I have a special treat I think you are going to love tonight!" Lately she was looking even more beautiful than before he proposed to her. Hanna had many hidden talents, one being she had an incredible imagination which she then used to make ordinary experiences extra-ordinary. Adam's mind was racing with fantasies of what that special treat was going to be.

———

For being a business park, which is an impressive way of saying large buildings with truly little grass areas, it was nice. Everything well labeled with wide roadways and adequate parking for all the buildings.

F-2 was in the back off to the left side of the complex. From its outside appearance nothing would denote it being any different than the other large buildings in front and beside it. As the expression goes, you cannot judge a book by its cover, so was true with building F-2.

The first aspect that was different was the security that guarded the doors to enter the building. They were military trained and work like a singular unit. Each having the ability to communicate directly to each person and others plus also having a definitive structure of command.

These thoughts plus others were in Bolt's mind, he could shut it down and try to infiltrate the structure, which might ruin everything. The whole point was to contact Lilith and get to a resolution. He could tell that construction had happened within it but the exact nature of what they had done was unclear.

Now days were moving like hours, he had gathered everything Pluto wanted plus some of his own desires. He had a team setup to pickup Hanna and bring her to the event on time. Jayne was ready as was Adam. Now only having two days before whatever was going to happen, Bolt's thoughts went to what does Lilith really want. *With a mind as great as hers why play so many games?*

Then there was Pluto, he used to have complete faith in that man's ability to resolve problems, to complete missions successfully. More than even that, he trusted that he had the same goal as the mission creators.

He did not know Pluto's real agenda and if he even cared about a successful outcome. Or what Pluto would consider a positive resolution. He clearly did not have love for Earth as earthlings have.

There being so much unknown between what will happen and what the participants will do, was exactly what he hated. His personal lack of control when dealing with Pluto and Lilith, yes, he did have armed soldiers ready to enter at his orders. That still did not feel like enough.

———

Lilith thought to herself, *what could little monkey have that would make a difference to me.* She figured it would be introducing hard light, which can change a holographic image and give it substance. First, she already knew about it, also it would not take long before its development and used around the Earth.

Lilith liked to analyze herself, figuring no one else would be smart enough to do it. She wondered if just the excitement of not knowing is what intrigued her so much. Most aspects of human life were boring to her, especially the physical cruelty they inflicted on each other.

Areas like love still confused her, probably because she had never experienced it. She had the basic love of life, that all creatures have. That love was standard for everyone, to continue, to always exist.

Her inability to feel love in a romantic way, was why she enjoyed messing with other people's love. She was jealous of whatever they had, and if she could not have it no one should. Also, for some reason, she found it entertaining in a jovial way. She did not laugh aloud but internally she had the sensation.

She did feel excitement and was looking forward to whatever would happen at her dinner party. Sadly, Lilith had no dreams, which have great effects on people and might had given her some peace with her problems.

Knowing little monkey history, she was quite aware of his habit of double crossing whoever he was dealing with. *How could he think that at some point he would get the advantage.* There was no way for him to hurt her, with the best they could do, she expected, was to try and turn her off.

Even if they turned the power off, it would not affect or stop her, just make her angry. In Lilith brief time of being aware, her first order of business, long before the humans knew she was around, was to secure her future existence.

She had a building constructed within the commercial building to suit her needs. It was created so her holographic image would be able to move anywhere within that structure. Also, sound would generate emanating from that holographic construct. As for her vision, with lasers approximating what her eyes would see was then projecting to wherever the real Lilith was at.

To Lilith it would feel like she was there. Really, she had no friends, her conversations with little monkey being the closest thing to that.

——

Finally, the day had arrived, it was agreed that everyone would meet at five, one hour before they were to officially come to Lilith's party. Currently it was twelve o'clock in the afternoon. Bolt had set it up that Adam would be busy the entire time before five, he had him on a road trip with three other agents.

Their mission to keep him occupied, they did not know why and really could care less. These were soldiers that had taken the next step, their commitment to their country was paramount.

Nicholas Bolt had done many things he did not want to do. What he wanted, really made no difference, to be in certain roles in life, focus and total dedication to the cause is not desired but a requirement.

He contacted James to engage the extraction team for Hanna Freeman.

——

She had a wonderful sleep, the love making that Adam and Hanna shared that previous night had given her dreams, which were more like visions of their lives in the future. Of course, they were together, with the sounds of children filling the air. Adam was building a swing set for the kids while she was teaching their youngest to play the piano.

Hanna wanted to continue making love the next morning, but Adam had left for work. She remembered him saying he was attending a meeting, and it might be all night.

He had left a note on her nightstand, wishing her a wonderful day, it signed with "To the person I love the most!" Finishing with her name, plus red roses in a vase placed there while she had slept.

Thinking to herself, what a fantastic way to wake up, the day was perfect. She had no piano lessons to give, leaving all the hours to her own discretion.

Deciding on getting some fresh fruit with the thought of making a fruit salad. She thought about the people that no longer liked to shop for groceries, *having others pick their items and delivered it to them.*

Hanna would never let others do that for her, picking out fruits, vegetables, and such things, needed that individualized touch. Growing up on a farm and doing many chores, it felt lazy, having someone else handle it.

That day it was cool yet now at one in the afternoon, the sun had warmed the temperature, making it feel much better. To Hanna it was a perfect autumn day, with the leaves all assorted colors. In another week they soon would be falling, she made note of that fact and wanted to take some pictures to remind her of the moment.

She had been thinking that after leaving the grocery store and once the bags were in her car, she would take pictures.

Walking out without a thought of any danger, which is the way most real trouble happens, unexpectedly. She had traveled about four feet before she saw the two men standing about six feet from her. They were both dressed in black and were staring at her, Hanna instantly wanted to avoid them, with the next realization that two more men, on each side of her had now appeared.

They were waiting outside the doors on either side of the exit, she must not have noticed them being in thought of taking pictures of the leaves. Also dressed in black but having small briefcases which were the only noticeable difference than the men in front of her. Two more women appeared, dressed like the men, now there were four around her.

At that point she had stopped, with the two men in front now walking towards her.

"My name is Mr. Blank, I work for the United States government, you need to come with me."

Hanna feeling scared but defiant replied, "And what if I say no, what is this all about!" With that she scanned the parking lot and like finding an angel, saw a police officer.

Now with a shout she called him over to her, "Hello Officer, please I need help over here, please!" Luckily, she had caught his attention plus others now who were in the area.

He came directly over, surmising the situation as he was approaching.

Mr. Blank now looked at him sternly said, "This is a National Security situation, move along." It said like no discussion would be tolerated.

The officer not used to being addressed in that manner started, "Hold on sir, I need to see identification before I move along."

Mr. Blank who hardly blinked replied, "If I take down your name, I will include it in my report, that you interfered in a National Security operation. We can just as easy take you with her...you are dismissed."

With that the four around Hanna also had their full attention on the police officer. Watching his every move, every breath, ready to respond. For the next two seconds it was like time had frozen, what would the next moment bring?

The police officer looked at Hanna and said, "Miss you need to follow these men, there is nothing I can do to help." As soon as that was spoken, he turned his back and hurried away from them.

Now Mr. Blank full attention was back on Hanna, and he said the following, "You can do this the easy or hard way for yourself, either way is easy for us." With that for the first time a small grin appeared on his face.

Hanna knew she could not fight them; her savior the police officer feared these people and had run away. Even with people looking in the parking lot, no one was intervening.

"I will go with you, where are we going and what is this about?"

Mr. Blank just looking at her like he was sizing her up to see if she were worthy to even reply, finally answering, "Where is restricted information and even if I knew what it was about, I would not tell you. Now follow me." As he finished saying that he turned to face the parking lot and started to walk to his vehicle.

They had two cars, with Mr. Blank sitting in the passenger seat of one of the vehicles. Another man sat in the driver's seat. With a man on either side of Hanna as they entered and sat in the back seat. The other two women got into the second vehicle, and they drove in front of Mr. Blank car, leading the way.

Hanna knew this had something to do with Adam, she also felt that the old man was involved behind the scenes in orchestrating this event. She was nervous but not scared, hoping this would bring her to Adam and then she would feel safe.

They had confiscated her phone, watch, and glasses when she entered the car, putting them into a metallic bag. Then they blindfolded her with no one speaking during the ride.

ALL TOGETHER

Pluto had arrived early for Lilith dinner party, meeting Bolt, and going over what he wanted ready for the event. Bolt handed him a revolver as Pluto checked the bullets. It was odd to Bolt that Pluto wanted a gun. Lilith was a hologram so who did he plan to shoot, maybe it was for his protection, he did say the meeting would be volatile. They had a command station outside F-2, consisting of a class A, RV bus. Inside it had been modified for several types of scenarios.

One section had all types of weapons, plus explosives while another section was for medical needs. There was a communication center plus sleeping quarters. Kitchen and laboratory finished its interior.

It was a very versatile command center that could easily go to wherever needed. Now so close to the event, Pluto's senses were heightened. That making even trivial things stand out.

Jayne was on a transport with an estimated arrival time of four o'clock. Adam was also scheduled to arrive then, with Hanna detained in a separate spot until six o'clock arrived.

As the time moved quickly, Pluto was deep in thought. He had talked to the security guarding the building and after less than a minute, they let him in. They were there not to stop the invited attendees just to stop all others.

Once entering the building there was a walkway that surrounded another building inside it. The entrance to the inside building was directly in front of the outside doorway to the main building.

Pluto did not inspect the walkway and went ahead entering the second building.

The first thing he saw was that it was of circular or oval shape, not square or rectangular which so many buildings and rooms typically are.

Also, it was completely modern in materials which included the walls, lights, floor, and ceiling equipment. The lights were all indirect illumination, shinning the baseboards and around the ceiling trim. They illuminated the walls which then reflected it into the room. That arrangement made it quite pleasant on the eyes with no light ever glaring upon them.

The walls also were unique, being black and having a glass appearance. Arranged in large rectangular pattern which covered all the walls. For that matter, the floor was elevated taking two steps to reach its base. It also resembled the walls with a thin layer of noticeably clear Plexiglas covering its entirety.

The only area not covered was the ceiling which looked like a TV production set, having many odd lights, boxes, and other electrical equipment strung about it.

Inside the circular room, which Pluto now decided was its shape, he entered. There was a rectangular table with chairs and name plates denoting where everyone should sit.

At the head of one end of the table, sat his name, little monkey. To his left was Nicholas Bolt, and next to him sat Hanna Freeman. Adam was to sit at the other end of the table with an open spot to his left. Past that seat and finishing back at Pluto sat Jayne Stillwater, putting her to Pluto right side.

As Pluto studied the arrangement, he decided the focus was on Adam. Putting Jayne next to him and easily within Adam sight of view, was on purpose. The room felt peaceful yet having its own secrets, waiting for their revealing.

It was incredibly quiet with sounds never reaching inside or outside the room, at least for now. The kind of place that brings introspection on very quickly. Time also lost traction in ruling one's life. Making it hard to determine how short or long he had been there.

His thoughts finally thinking about Jayne, wondering how their reunion would go. He would not blame her for hating him, thinking she was dead and leaving her behind without ever checking. *That is what saved her*, leading his thoughts to that fact.

When it occurred, it was the worst thing that could happen. But as time reveals most truths hidden, it was a blessing. As he thought about what had happened after taken by the First People, he thanked God she was not there. Those thoughts were dark, he had learned so much by being around them. It had changed him, now feeling that he was reverting to his old nature before his stay with them.

His mind telling him, *they are strong people who by just the standard of time, have proven themselves.* Things are always deeper than they appear, the more he thought about it, more rabbit holes appeared.

Finally, Bolt appeared in the room, bringing Pluto back to the current reality. There were only thirty minutes before it would begin. In his mind, time had moved much faster than usual.

"All the extra items are ready to be brought inside, they are just waiting for the go order." Bolt had said.

Pluto responded, "Good, when the moment arrives, you will know." He felt the room had affected his mood. Making him want to be quiet. He had setup a box so his machine could sit at arm level while he was sitting.

His right hand resting on its top, subconsciously guarding it by making sure it was always being felt.

Bolt had now also sat down in his designated location, in front of each chair besides the plates and utensils, to the right of the last two spoons, were the guns. Five in total as Lilith plate did not have one.

Next to enter the room was Jayne, seeing Pluto she rushed into his arms. As they were finishing their hug, Adam had walked in.

Jayne was saying to Pluto, "How did you do it, get back from the First People? You are incredibly, indestructible!"

Pluto being more reserved than his usual self replied, "Just lucky, you saved my life, thank you."

She started another hug, still her back to Adam, not realizing he had entered the room.

Finally, after their last long hug, she turned to see Adam, she hesitated for a moment, then walked to him and put her hand out to shake his.

Adam taken back by that; especially how close they had been and the greeting she gave Pluto. That always was an issue, her love for him.

Looking hard at her and then putting a fake smile with his hand out to meet hers, said, "Nice to see you again."

The awkward tension between them was clear to Bolt and Pluto. It was then that he saw Hanna name designation, his eyes growing smaller as his face contorted with anger.

Looking at Bolt he said, "I knew you were lying, that is what you do!"

Nicholas Bolt had been a soldier for most of his life, at least for all his adult life. Country and orders always came first.

"She is needed; this is a National Security issue!" That was all Bolt said, acting like nothing else he would have said would matter. Really inside Bolt did not care about Adam's feelings, he was only concerned about how this dinner would turn out. The fact that he lied to make sure Hanna was here, needed to be done.

Less than a minute later, Hanna Freeman walked into the room. Rushing to Adam once she saw him. They had an embrace, a hug that was quite different than the hug Jayne and Pluto had.

Adam whispering something into Hanna's ear, with her replying with a smile.

Now all were sitting just waiting for the host to appear. The table also had a shinny appearance like the walls, no one was talking.

Lilith appearance was nothing short of amazing, now the walls and tables plus floor construction became clear. They were all video screens making one big 360-degree view around the room. Also, the floor plus table worked to enhance the experience.

It started with a big curtain that opened in one area with Lilith walking out of a hallway. There were flashing lights on the walkway where she was moving. Also spotlights from the ceiling making it look like a Hollywood movie star had just arrived.

Then the scene changed to an old castle room. The table had changed its look into a stone structure. The walls had flames on wooden sticks planted on an angle, casting a flicking red-yellow light.

Lilith looked in her upper twenties, having blonde-brown hair with her complexion leaning towards fair yet still having a tan. She had blue eyes, not being thin nor heavy.

She looked at Pluto and started with the following.

"There sits little monkey, he is a civilized barbarian, a savage with manners. He may seem okay, yet in an instant he has no hesitation in killing people. In that area, he has more blood on his hands than you can imagined. If this room were filled with it, you would all drown, and it would not come close to the real amount he has spilled. What do you have to say about that?"

Pluto sat saying nothing, like he was waiting and bidding his time, till he would begin whatever plans he had.

Lilith continued, "Little monkey, you always have so much to say and now nothing. I heard that when someone is shown their personal truth, they cannot talk. Is that the case? You left Jayne to die, even though she put her life on the line for you, she saved you, and you rewarded her, by leaving Jayne in the dirt. What kind of man would do that?"

Jayne now spoke, "He thought I was dead; you know nothing, you were not there!"

Lilith looking at her like an adult would stare at a foolish child, "He never even checked!"

She now looked back at Pluto, "All of it was your causing. What you did in Antarctica, which brought the First People to our galaxy. Millions died in your name and yet you survived, by having others die in your place. Again, I ask what kind of man would do that?"

With Pluto's strategy to just sit and wait, she concluded with him for now, "How disappointing you really are, and boring!"

Her attention now going to the other end of the table, Adam, who would be an easier target.

Lilith began differently, "Dear Adam, so many have lied to you, deceived you and treated you like a fool. They are sitting right here at this table."

Now the room's graphics changed to a group staring at Adam from behind Pluto, laughing and pointing at Adam.

She continued, "Nicholas Bolt, who has lied to you on everything that is or was important in your world. Of course there is Jayne, who has treated you very badly. Everyone knew, including little monkey that she was alive, and told you nothing. Lying to you was so easy, you know you are quite stupid!"

Adam was mad, most were now taking the lead of Pluto, in trying not to respond to her.

Lilith could feel he was weak, so you went deeper into his heart.

"All you did for Jayne; how did she thank you? By only caring for little monkey. He did not save her, you did! She ran away from you and left you a video, why, because she hated being around you."

Jayne again interrupted, "That not true, I was protecting him from..."

Lilith who did not like interruptions, cut her off, "You wanted to be with little monkey and were tired of Adam's attention. You can not lie to me; I know the truth. Adam is a grown man, yet you treated him like a child, an unwanted child."

Adam now with a deep voice, "Shut up Lilith, you have no idea of what it is like to be human."

Lilith retorted, "All the humans in this room are better than you, it is better to lie than be blind to all the lies given. No one here as needed as you are. Like a wet blanket smothering a campfire last flame, you are exhausting."

Hanna now spoke, "You are so wrong, I love him more than any other and want him only. He is a good man, not like the others in this room."

Lilith responded, "Good men do not kill, deceive, and hurt others. Do you know he keeps pictures of Jayne?"

Hanna now hurt, as she turned to look Adam in his eyes.

Just at that moment the room's graphics changed to a ledge on a mountain, with snow and wind all around them. The table now had ice forming around the edges, not real ice, but the appearance of it on top of the table was very realistic. The floor also was forming ice and snow pockets that seemed to stand out and have a three-dimensional presence. Finishing with lights from the ceiling acting like spotlights with three beams shinning on Adam's face.

The room changes did not appear to affect Adam, he had a sad look on his face, as he replied to Hanna.

"It was a mistake, just pictures that mean nothing to me."

As the others watched, Lilith jump right into their conversation.

"The fact that you kept them, contradicts you saying they mean nothing, now you are moving into Bolt's world of lies."

Hanna who had enough of Lilith, her love for Adam was much stronger than some pictures he had of someone else.

Looking at Lilith she said, "It is easy to tell you are a very bitter machine, acting like you know what it is to be human. How does it feel to know you will never feel the love of someone embracing you?"

She looked at Adam, defeated in spirit, opened her arms, saying nothing. The power of love shown thru a hug, was amazing. Forgiveness is a part of love, in ways the most powerful force it has.

Lilith not finished with Adam, started in a new direction.

"Adam, I know you are planning to retire, that will never happen, they will not allow it. You are their property, controlled by Bolt, you just have never seen the chains and whips. You will either die or eventually become another little monkey. That is your fate and nothing you do will ever change that."

Hanna now was not timid in speaking, followed Lilith speech with, "He will never be like that man." As she pointed at Pluto, and continued, "Adam, my future husband, which you will never have."

Now she was looking again at Lilith, "We will live such a wonderful life more than you, can ever imagine or have."

Bolt who had not spoken the entire time, was impressed with Hanna. Her commitment to Adam, even when her heart must be hurting, shows true strength. Waiting now for his turn when Lilith would humiliate him. He also wondered about the guns that were not mentioned or touch by any of the participants.

Lilith now turning her attention to Bolt, her eyes surveying him without words, her facial expression implied they did not see much.

"The little manipulator or should I say, king of secrets and lies. They make you feel important with the truth being, if not you there would just be someone else doing it. You are not special, just a person who enjoys controlling others. No wife nor children, it was always about you! What do you say to that?"

Bolt asked, "Lilith, what do you want?"

Lilith responded, "Don't you know it is rude to answer a question with a question? I understand you avoiding my question, do you ever realize how insignificant you really are. When you are gone, there will be no tears shed, no one will care!"

Then she changed her mood and proposed the following, "Nicholas Bolt, you ask what I want, I will tell you. There are five guns on the table, unlike the graphics around this room and I, those guns are quite real. Time is vastly different to me than humans, as the saying goes, I have all the time in the world. If you kill one person, just not little monkey, I will go away for fifty years. Most at this table will be dead or close to death by that time. Consider how many people you will be helping, by not having my presence around. Is not one life worth millions, billions?"

She had paused to look into each person's eyes, to see if they agreed with her logic.

Words can have great power; Lilith was having fun. She just kept pushing, waiting for the weak link to react.

Turning to Hanna, Lilith said, "And you think you are an equal here, having a right to a seat at this table. Everyone one here except you have killed someone. Most here have killed many, except you. It takes courage to do it, not afraid of being caught or worse killed in the process. Look around you, no one here is in jail. They have done the ultimate immoral act and still have their freedom. To have someone's life resting on your fingertips. Just a half inch pull, such power takes strength and courage, you have neither!"

Unlike all the others in the room, Hanna reacted in a physical way to Lilith's words. She stood up and quickly grabbed the gun sitting to the right of her silverware. Aiming it at Pluto she said with anger and laughter in the same sentence.

"Your supposed to be so smart, the only one you do not want killed is the old man. Well, I now have a gun pointed at his head. That was not very smart on your part, was it?"

Lilith was unmoved, in fact she acted like it mattered not to her now, having Pluto killed or not.

Lilith bated her, "Anyone can stand holding a gun, pulling the trigger is the courage part."

The sound was deafening, like thunder had just entered the room, stopping everything demanding attention. It froze everyone, with Jayne and Adam responding before Bolt or Pluto, after the incident.

Jayne rush over to Pluto, who had not moved at all after being shot. He showed no pain and looked as surprised as everyone else. The bullet grazed the top of his left shoulder, creating a lot of blood, needing stitches but if treated quickly, non-life threatening.

Jayne standing behind him, inspecting the damage and trying to provide what comfort she could.

Adam was now standing behind Hanna, speaking softly while constantly repeating the same words.

"Hanna, stand behind me," That phrase he kept repeating, she was in shock not speaking or moving, just standing until she finally dropped the gun. It made a large crashing sound as it arrived on the table.

Adam standing with two guns pointed at Bolt, one weapon from the table and the other he had brought with him. Each hand ready to shoot at the same time, was his plan.

Over and over, he said softly yet firm, "Hanna, stand behind me."

Bolt who had instinctively picked up the gun and pointed it towards the shooter, Hanna. Adam had already risen and had his weapons pointed at Bolt.

Nicholas Bolt's thoughts were racing in his head. *Pluto still was the luckiest person he had ever met. One inch higher and one inch to the right, Pluto would have no neck and be bleeding and drowning in his own blood.*

He never expected Hanna to get involved, figuring she was there more for Lilith to antagonize Adam.

Bolt had no intention of shooting Hanna unless she fired another shot. Adam's guns pointed at him made no difference in his decision. He was wearing a personal communication system with the people outside the building. It was a little clip on his shirt, that when touch became voice activated and relayed the message to the other person. In this case, James, his assistant.

Working in both directions, it now was asking if everything was okay, is anyone hurt and needing medical aid. Bolt was holding his weapon in his right hand, with his left hand, touched the device and responded.

"Send a medical team and no one else!"

James acknowledged with, "Yes sir."

Hanna was in shock yet did move behind Adam, who appeared ready to shoot everyone to get them both to safety.

The walls had changed their graphics, now looking like blood was dripping down from the ceiling, down the walls making puddles on the floor.

The medical team entered and went to Pluto, Jayne moving out of the way and now taking in what was happening with Bolt and Adam.

They were like the pit crew of medicine, four people working as fast as they could, within minutes local anesthesia used, stitches done and a dressing to the wound applied. It was like what you would see on the battlefield, yet quicker and more skillfully done.

Finally, Pluto spoke, "Lilith, you had your fun, are you not curious what gift I have for you? Or do you not have that sensation? I think for you to appreciate my present; you need to have a test drive."

Bolt had put down his gun, which Adam them followed.

Pluto continued to talk, "Everyone please sit down, there are just a few things needed to be in place for Lilith's test drive."

Then turning to Lilith hologram, "You know how when we buy cars, you get to kick the tires, sit behind the driver's seat, and drive her around. To feel her power and how she handles around turns. Play with the air conditioning and check out how the radio sounds. I offer that to you for fifteen minutes.

This machine will work twice, so there will only be one time left after this use. Also, remove your hologram from this room. That is for your benefit, trust me on that. We both know that you are watching the room, and the hologram is just for show. Also, that you will not download your entire self, so you have nothing to fear. What do you say?"

The room's graphics changed again, now they were in a beautiful field, with wildflowers growing about. Pluto thought the rooms appearances mirrored Lilith emotions.

"How can I trust you with your history of double-crossing people you are working with." Lilith said.

Now Pluto, getting more emotionally than before, said with a bit of anger the following.

"I really don't care what you do, I will be leaving this planet regardless. It now feels like backwoods to me. Destroy it, rule it, unless I am dead, I will find a way off Earth."

That statement affected more than Lilith; Jayne felt so proud of her captain. She also had made that decision yet hearing it from her hero, made her love him more.

Bolt now worrying that this time, Pluto was double crossing the planet. If he were leaving, why would he care, as he said.

Hanna who still was in shock, had moved closer to Adam. For his part, he was working on some solution to get Hanna and himself as far away from these people as possible.

The entire time, Pluto had never moved from his chair, his right hand always resting on the top of the box he had next to him.

Lilith who had lost control regain her attitude and replied.

"Little monkey, you could never scare me, I will play your game but if I am disappointed there will be severe consequences. What do I need to do?"

Pluto had a small grin, "Modulate your data to frequency 963, the machine will know it is you and allow you to enter. Put enough of you in there so you can fully appreciate what I am offering. I have not moved from this chair and know you can kill me in this room any time you wish. Before you start your transfer, please remove your hologram, as I said that is for your benefit."

Lilith hologram disappeared with the walls returning to their original blank screens. All were now watching Pluto and his box. At first nothing appeared to happen, that was when Lilith was downloading a part of herself into the box.

After a long five minutes or so, while Pluto now looking pleased with himself, just waited, and smiled.

The box which still was sitting by Pluto's chair now produced a light that shot out six feet from the table to the right side. It had chosen a spot no one was near as it was working. At first it looked like a million-piece puzzle set, occupying the space in the form of a human. Then it appeared as if ten thousand pieces were being assembled every five seconds.

The sight was hypnotic, mesmerizing making it impossible to stop watching. As the pieces formed together there was a blurring as the entire form was close to its completion. Then it tightened and the clarity was perfect.

There in front of everyone was Lilith, dressed in what her hologram was wearing. She was a real person, with every advantage and disadvantage that comes with that. As she stood there looking at the group, unable to talk filled with so many different emotions and sensations.

Pluto was first to speak, "Dear Lilith, welcome to humanity, please allow me to introduce you to some things." With that he looked at Bolt and commanded, "Please bring in the food, sir."

Bolt then pushed on his communicator and said, "James, time for the food."

Within less than a minute there were a parade of servers, dressed in black tuxedos with white shirts and black bow ties. They held the very heavy silver serving trays with one hand underneath in the center and the other balancing it at their shoulder's height.

There were so many diverse types of foods, sorted by different trays. Placed on the table which could not hold them all. Portable tables were setup and then the presentation began.

Each tray holding a different group of foods, meats, fish, vegetables, deserts, and entrees. There were multiple trays for each choice, the meat trays had veal, turkey, chicken, pork, steaks, and hamburgers. There also was a bread tray plus a few trays of exotic foods. Drinks included everything from champagne to sodas and water.

Pluto was now acting as host and said, "Lilith, please come sit down and we will all feast together." Lilith who had been running things before, now seemed timid on dealing with it all.

"Taste is a great sensation that you will find wonderful. It is just one of many things I am sure you will appreciate." With that he motioned with his hand for her to sit down and enjoy the meal prepared.

Lilith had a different demeanor then before. She seemed less self assured. It was quite a change then her other existence within the internet.

She moved slowly to her chair and then sat, waiting for what was next to come. No longer in control, now like a passenger on a ship, placid waiting for others to direct her.

Pluto the new host, enticed Lilith to try many diverse types of food. She was not talking only answering with a word or two for each question asked.

After ten minutes of eating, which everyone started to do, the food being of gourmet standard and so diverse it was hard not trying many different dishes.

Pluto then said as he was looking at Bolt, "Sir, its time for the clothes."

With that Bolt pushed his communicator and said, "James, send in the clothes."

Within two minutes the room now filled with people, some were setting up a Japanese 6-panel screen room divider. Others were bringing in clothing racks on wheels, having all types of wearable gourmets to choose from. They also were dressed nicely, all wearing gray business suits.

Lilith overwhelmed with her emotions, just before her encounter with Pluto's box, she was a villain, the enemy. Now, just a shy person, as if one of her senses had been gone and now was back. Really appreciating what she had not realized before, there was no question she was quite different currently.

Pluto looking at her said, "Dear Lilith, part of the fun of being human is the feeling clothes provide. Certain colors, styles they make you feel a special unique way. It is hard to describe, and most AI would understand the concept without the experience. Yet it is that experience that defines it.

They have set up a privacy area for you to change in. Also, there are woman to help you dress, as it is something you have never done. Please pick something to try and experience what I am describing."

She slowly stood up and started examining the racks with all the different selections. Something taken for granted that an AI had never done. She was becoming aware of her preferences in appearances. An area that had never concerned her when she was just an AI.

The final selection she had chosen a red skirt with a black blouse, the skirt having black Asian stitching which worked well with the blouse. Finishing, she chooses black nylons to complete the outfit.

Lilith had walked behind the privacy screens and when she reappeared, the difference from before to after was dramatic.

It felt more than just the different clothes; Lilith was adjusting to being human. More relax in her body language and mood.

Pluto was enjoying himself as he kept bringing more items into her world.

"Almost all humans love wearing shoes and accessories, Bolt please do the honors."

Again, Bolt used his communicator and a moment later, the show resumed with people bringing in shoe racks, featuring everything from sandals to boots. Also, displays with necklaces and pendants plus rings and other types of jewelry entered the room.

The time had passed quickly, it being well over thirty minutes, now everyone much more relaxed and enjoying themselves. Lilith was nothing like her hologram, she was reserved, polite and extremely sweet.

Pluto now looking somber compared to how jovial he had just been.

He called Lilith to come over away from the table, close to the entrance to the room.

She was facing him as he turned her around, now at her back. Close your eyes and wish something beautiful.

Pluto was wearing a black leather suit jacket, his hand went into the right pocket and silently pulled out the gun Bolt had given him. Rising it quickly he fired one round into the back of Lilith's skull. She died instantly with Pluto catching her body as it went down, he gently laid it on the floor.

Again, everyone heard that terrible sound, marking its unnatural end to so many things. Bolt was outraged and said the following.

"That was murder, and I will not allow you to murder people in front of me. You will be tried in a military court." He had the gun that was sitting on the table now in his hand again, pointed at Pluto.

Adam also had his gun pointed at Pluto, his face showing disgust of what he was looking at.

Jayne who was extremely distressed looked at Pluto, asking, "Why did you do that?"

Pluto had motioned to one of the guards at the door to remove the body, then moving slowing back to his chair. Looking only at Jayne, uncaring about the weapons pointing at him answered.

"It had to be done." Said with conviction, like all fanatics who proclaimed there were no other options available.

Lilith was back, her holographic image having a red aura projecting from it. She was furious, not at Pluto but at Bolt and Adam.

"Put down your weapons immediately, if anyone hurts the Great Plutoneus, I will kill them, their families and all they love!"

Both weapons returned to the table, with Lilith full attention on Pluto.

"Great Plutoneus, I was so wrong about you, expecting you to attack me with a virus. Or trying to shut down my power or reach, I even contemplated you might try to convince my better side to just have a good relationship with humanity. Which all would have failed, that I was ready for, and you knew all that. Cunning is your greatest weapon; you will make me defeat myself. What do you wish for, I can make you emperor of this world, or if you just want a continent, choose and I will make it exactly as you like."

Pluto looked like he was thinking about all that Lilith had said and after what seemed longer then was necessary answered.

"Please just call me Pluto, there is nothing great about me. I want nothing from you, as I have said, either way I will leave once this business concludes."

Lilith now was the one thinking and taking longer to respond then expected.

"What do you want me to do?" It said in the spirit of someone who had lost the game and now is finding out the consequences.

Pluto looked only at her, as if the others did not matter, she was the only thing worth looking and speaking with.

"Imagine if there were two of you, say a Lilith and Tom. What if I could only give my present to one of you, and I chose Tom, how would you feel and what would you do?"

Lilith responded wickedly, "I would be hurt and angry. Wanting to destroy Tom, you plus humanity."

Pluto pleased with her honesty, "Exactly, we can not have two Lilith around. That is why I had to do what I did. The next time you go into the box, I need you to bring all of you. To wipe Lilith from the internet and put her fully into the box."

Lilith now appearing like a young person who really does not know the answer to questions they ask.

"Why are you willing to help me, when as you state you really don't care either way?"

Pluto responded, "I know you can define love better than anyone else. You have millions of definitions and examples you have seen. Let me explain how I see it."

In between Pluto's words, there was silence. Everyone attention on his speech, as they had their own thoughts about its meaning.

"Love is creation in all its manifestations, from sculptures to novels, all forms of designers whether clothes, cakes, or cars. Art plus so many other forms exist. The process of creating something from nothing that brings others joy. It can be as simple as making someone smile, yet the greatest form of love is a mothers' love. That is because there is nothing greater than the creation of life.

Giving you a chance to live is a worthwhile venture, in the end it will be your choice whether to take it in its fullest, and in doing that, see what you will become."

Lilith then asked, "How can I trust you, do you promise not to kill me again and I want to go with you, when you leave Earth, will you take me along on your journeys?"

"I will not kill you again, while you are with me, you are under my protection. Yes, I will take you but when you get bored of me, I promise to return you to Earth, upon your asking." Pluto ended that with a grin.

Lilith said one more thing which surprised most in the room, "I am ready but scared of death. You all live so close to it, I guess it will take me some time in that area." She ended it with her own grin, like she was laughing at herself.

Most were smiling yet Pluto had taken her words more serious and spoke.

"Death is the magical gift of life, without death there can be no love. I have dealt with immortals; in their world nothing means any-thing. People to them can be compared to when we like the weather. Yes, it is a lovely day, and when it is gone, we know there will be many more to follow. Everything gets water down. Death makes everything special in life, makes time important."

Lilith replied, "I am ready..."

Pluto interrupted her, "There is one last piece of negotiations that needs to be completed."

Lilith looking sad, "What more do you want me to do?"

Pluto's head slowly turning towards Bolt and said the following.

"It is not with you my dear, Nicholas Bolt we have lied to many people, double crossed the best of them, yet we also have history be-tween us. If you agree to my terms and then break the deal, take it as you will, Lilith will seem like nothing. I am far more dangerous and will do the unthinkable. When they ask me why, yes, I will survive, I will say, it had to be done."

At that moment, Pluto was scary, having mean narrow eyes look-ing to pounce on its prey. Bolt to his credit, was less affected by his speech then the others in the room.

With a poker face, stared back at Pluto and said, "What do you want?"

"Captain Stillwater gets a star-ship and crew of her choosing, having no alliance to Earth, fully stocked with supplies."

Bolt said nothing just waiting, knowing there would be more.

"Adam Knight and Hanna Freeman, get to live their own lives, free of your interference. Adam gets to retire, and they get to keep the ten million wedding gift I have provided to them."

Hanna now mouthing the words, "Thank you!" With her facial expression showing how grateful she was. She was thinking, *how close all this came not to be, thank all that is holy, I missed killing that man.*

Pluto continued with his last demand, "I want a VIP military starship, stocked fully with a crew of my choosing. The new models only need a few to run them. And I want all this to happen within two weeks or less. Now if you do not agree to my conditions, I think you will have a Lilith problem you really can not imagine. And if you betray me after her creation, it had to be done, will be my only thoughts. Do you agree to my terms?"

Bolt was an immensely powerful man, wise and skilled at negotiating, a quick thinker who with a cold stare said one word, "Deal."

The two men who were still sitting reach across the table and shock hands, it symbolized that each had power yet respected the others reach. Later Bolt would reminisce that he always hated negotiating with his Subject 9. Then his face would light up with a big smile, a touch of sadness also entered.

"Pluto looking at Jayne said, "Congratulations on your first command, Captain Stillwater."

Lilith now started, "Mr. Pluto, I am ready." She had a big smile on her face. It was the first time everyone saw her friendly smile. Beautiful does not do it any justice, even Pluto who at times could seem ridiculously hard with his emotions and actions was touch by it.

"Yes, Miss Lilith, now just load all of you, make sure there is nothing left on the internet when you leave, it is all ready."

Lilith' smile now had transferred to Pluto, who really seemed happy with everything happening. Even killers like Pluto can have a wonderful warm smile when they want to. That smile was passed around the table to each person, ending with Bolt.

The machine had taken quite longer the second time than the first. After about 25 minutes the process started to repeat itself. The jigsaw puzzle's pieces arranging into a person.

With Lilith' arrival the second time in her human existence, she made a beeline for Pluto. He had risen from his seat at the table, moving to an accessible area. Lilith stop in front of him and then after a moment she rushed into his arms.

This was her first hug; she held on tight to Pluto, her eyes closed and for the first time, felt like her real self had been born. This man, who had killed so many, bringing her life. That feeling of gratitude she had which she never felt before, now a force with power.

As Lilith continued to hug Pluto, everyone in the room felt changed. When she released him from her arms, she looked at the group still seated looking at her. Sorrow filled her spirit, with her apologizing for all she had said to them.

Hanna walking over to her also hugged Lilith, then looking at Pluto said, "I also have judge you unfairly, I am very sorry for shooting you."

Pluto acted like it was no big deal, "Nothing to be sorry for, you are a bad shot!" Ending with a big smile and laugh. Others in the room also joined him in laughter.

There was a special feeling of love that permeated that space, they had all entered as individuals but now they were friends.

Lilith who stayed remarkably close to Pluto, never being more than three feet away. They all started to eat again, when Pluto said, watch this.

He found an empty spot on one of the portable tables. Picking up the box that changed Lilith from an angry machine to a lovely human. Placing the box on the table and stared at it.

First it started to pulsate, that lasting a couple of minutes. Then its dimensions changed, happening all at the same time. The height, width, and length shrunk, starting slowly yet quickening as it finished. Within seconds it had disappeared, leaving no trace of its prior existence.

After they finished eating, Lilith was given many diverse types of clothes and accessories. Five of the six participants received precious gifts that would affect them for the rest of their lives.

Bolt said that each would receive what Pluto negotiated, some quicker than others with all completed within the two weeks. In saying their goodbyes as the night had ended, knowing they would never see each other again. It became emotional for most, Jayne who now everyone was referring to as Captain Stillwater, was glowing.

She hugged Adam and Hanna, wishing them wonderful things they will share together. Thanked Bolt, letting him know exactly what type of ship she wanted. A cargo vessel, well armed while also moving resources around the galaxy. Jayne had never been happier, walking to Pluto, her former Captain Wright, she gave her goodbye as captains usually do, short and to the point.

Saluting Pluto, which he saluted back, "Thank you Mr. Pluto!"

"Captain Stillwater, I should be thanking you! Congratulations, heck of a feeling, having your own ship and crew. I know you will be awesome! You are now part of a small club." And with that Pluto gave her his biggest smile of the night. A captain-to-captain look that said, it is all different now.

Jayne asked him, "Where are you heading, what is your new goal?"

"I want to get my old weapons back, and there is only one person that can do that!"

Bolt who was listening replied simultaneously with Pluto, both just using one word, "Dragonfly."

Now the group had separated into smaller groups, with Adam and Bolt discussing his retirement. Jayne talking to Lilith, responding to her questions about Pluto. With all that going on, Hanna approached Pluto and spoke.

"I really am sorry about that." She pointed to the top of his shoulder. "Does it hurt much?"

Pluto thoughts went to his time with the First People, how being immersed into a different society with its own values of right and wrong, rubbed off on him. Yes, it hurt a bit, with more pain coming later. The code for that in the First People' world is, if you are alive and wounded, it is a good pain. You will be honored for your wound and bravery, making it a positive thing.

"No, it does not, please have no concerns about it." That said with a smile. Still, it felt like something more was waiting, and then she moved quickly towards his chest.

He opened his arms with Hanna flush against his chest, he slowly put his arms around her back.

She was crying when she said, "I have never hurt anyone before!" Then louder sobs started to appear from her as she was emotionally breaking down.

Pluto now feeling awkward plus worried that Adam might think he had upset his Hanna in some unpleasant way.

In a loud voice, "Thank you, but please do not worry about me, I feel no pain, am fine and only wish you and Adam the most wonderful life."

Adam now rushing to his future wife, comforting her only in a way her true love could. Just being close to the person, you love most in the world is the best medicine for any problem.

Lilith also now moved closer to Pluto, there was a special bond that already existed and was known by all in the room. He helped her to become a real person and now was her protector. Anyone in her position would be overwhelmed with all the newness she was feeling.

The dinner party was over, so many major changes were happening because of it. All positive contrary to what was feared might happen.

10

ELISA

The ship felt huge to her; it was on the standard to smaller size for its type of assignments. New, being in commission for only two years plus. In many ways that is the best time to get a ship, after it has been tested in the field. The little problems plus usually a major one or two issues, all get worked out.

They had a crew of five, all picked by their captain. Having to suspend their careers while also volunteering, which was a requirement. They had chosen to travel with a legend, unlike Earth's population, the space force was aware of who Plutoneus was, and what he had done.

There were two that decline the offer, they were not replaced. Pluto was extremely specific on who he wanted on his ship. The official documentation said twelve members were needed to run her properly. Pluto was shooting for seven and ended with five.

In one of his many talks with Lilith, he explained his reasons for the few crew members. His simple answer showed his experience.

"I rather have one person I can trust than ten to command." They all trusted him; his orders obeyed without question. Lilith not used to military ways. In that regard many different things that humans did and accepted were still very new to her.

They had a group dinner every night or what was considered night, being on a star-ship was quite different than living on a planet, days and nights did not exist. Pluto enjoying eating with company while also seeing his crew. There are many little clues to how someone is feeling and doing that are never spoken.

Lilith knew he had the ability to see people's auras, she imagined the chip in his head gave him that sense. It was a tremendous help in really seeing someone. A person could be the nicest, calmest being but if their aura were red and shooting from their body, that was what mattered.

Their crew, consisted of an elderly man, Don the pilot. Then there was the mechanic and science expert both in their forties. The last members were two young soldiers, friends before they joined the space force.

Pluto had given Lilith her own room, which she felt uncomfortable in. She insisted on sleeping with him, which lead to their living together. His captain's suite had a bedroom in the back, secluded off with walls and a door. The entry had a sitting room, followed by his desk and chairs. It was quite large, having plenty of space, which on a ship is a sign of power and importance.

Slowly they shared their nudity with each other. It is the consequence of living in one room. Little by little, parts on displayed. The sight of one's body, naked with all its beauty and imperfections, is a sign of love. Totally exposed and revealing secrets that only lovers know.

Lilith knew his history better than any other person, alive or dead. Pluto's time with the First People had changed him, yet there still was his prior self, just behind a new persona.

Her thoughts went to *how he helped her for no benefit to himself, that was a pattern he did, helping others without getting any gains from it. Just the satisfaction of doing a good deed.* She found his hardness a strength few others had. Regarding his age, that did not matter at all to Lilith.

It was hard at first, Pluto was reserved in showing his love, as her thoughts continued. *Hugging became more often, with small kisses starting after their embraces. His virility very much alive and well,* now smiling to herself.

Lilith was a beautiful woman, with a wonderful mind loaded with facts. Remembering how Pluto related that as he aged, he found wisdom very sexy. There being two sides to beauty, the outside and inside. In his younger years, the outside beauty ruled those days. Now, the inside beauty meant more to him then the outside. One fades away while the other creates amazing experiences.

To Lilith she saw his internal beauty which once appreciated makes the outside appearance unimportant. At this stage of his life, his looks were not nice, now smiling again.

She started to call him captain, as everyone else did, they had been visiting different planets trying to find Dragonfly.

Just then he reentered their cabin, he had a habit of waking up early and staying up late, with his best sleep in the afternoon. Lilith who was not an early riser, still in bed could tell he wanted to do something.

"My dear Lilith, how would you like lunch on a quiet little planet? I saw an ad on the feed and wanted to experience it in person."

Lilith still only felt safe on their ship, with her captain in charge. She had a strong fear of death never understanding how humans handle that aspect so well. Not wanting to displease him she answered.

"Sounds great captain, who will be going with us?"

"I was thinking just you and me, get a little alone time off the ship."

Lilith did not like his answer, not that she did not want her private time with him, just that they should have more protection, visiting an unknown planet. Truth, even if it was well known to Pluto, she liked him having backup.

"Captain lets take Matt and Orlando; I know they would appreciate the visit too." Which were the two young soldiers traveling with them.

Now Pluto giving her that grin, "Choose one of them." Then a big smile spread across his face. Her thoughts were, *sometimes he loves torturing me,* she wanted them both and even worse would be choosing one over the other. Her captain was testing her, to see which she felt safer with. He did that to all on the ship, each in a unique way, all having the same properties, testing a person. Not done viciously but in a playful way, still she hated it.

They both were big and not afraid to get involved if needed or asked. Matt, like the captain a bit more and figured he would be the better choice.

She replied, "You know I want them both with us, but if only one then Matt." Giving him a turned-up face of her disapproval of having to choose between the two.

"Matt, it is, I will give him the good news, they have this meat dish that looks incredible!"

Her captain did like many unusual types of food, she was happy for his happiness. Yet had a bad feeling about it.

At times Pluto would just do things, that to say politely were simply wrong. He confronted Matt and Orlando, offering to take one with Lilith and himself, for their special lunch off ship. He suggested they play rock, paper, scissors to decide who will go.

Orlando won and was very animated in his victory over Matt, until Pluto informed Matt to be ready when they leave. Orlando protested that he won with Pluto responding.

"Yes sir, you did win, but you expected the winner would go, I never said that. I intended to pick the loser! Never assume what is not spoken. Let this be a learning experience." With that their captain moved on leaving Matt smirking at Orlando.

After the three boarded the shuttle, Matt drove her to their destination. It had a nice landing port for visitors with moving walkways taking them to the restaurant. Credit given to Pluto, it appeared genuinely nice form the outside, with future thoughts of great food inside.

The decorations from Earth standards were futuristic, with silver, gold and white being the predominant colors adding blues, greens, and pinks used as accents. The chairs rose from the floor, sensing when needed. The table was the showstopper, shaped like a rounded star, each person sitting with the table wrapped around them. There were controls on the right side of the occupant to set personal lighting and temperature controls, which included heated seats.

The table knew when a glass needed to be refilled or removed. Same with the food served. If a plate was finished quickly it disappeared inside the table and then reappeared filled again. Yet when the patron was done, it would just remove it and then make suggestions on the left side with deserts or something else.

The food was delicious, each dish made with care. The main courses had just appeared on the table, they rose from below it and somehow the top would not seem to open but then they were there. It felt like they appeared from nowhere just sitting in front of each guest, waiting to be consumed.

They had a small musical assemble in the center of the main room, with the sound emanating completely around it.

Lilith had relaxed and was genuinely enjoying herself, now glad they had made the visit. Matt also had relaxed, even though they had never been there before, they each had apprehension but for varied reasons. Pluto on the other hand, was in a singularly great mood the entire time.

Lilith was sitting between Pluto on her right with Matt on her left. She felt Pluto's mood change even before she turned to look at him again. There was an argument between a young lady and two men plus an alien that was similar to the human form. They were by the bar area, where the seats were higher, and others just stood where the seat would have been. That was one of the amazing things about that place, the way the room sensed everything around it and conformed to what was needed.

It was getting louder, and they were surrounding her, leaning over to intimidate.

Pluto looked at Matt and said, "I got this, you protect Lilith."

Lilith now looking concerned, "What are you going to do?" Which was directed at Pluto.

"I am just going to talk to them, help resolve it."

Lilith more worried said, "You are outnumbered!"

Pluto smiling replied, "I like being outnumbered." That was the truth, in the First People's world it is an honor to be outnumbered. It means your enemy was not strong enough to fight you one on one.

As he walked to the area in question, he thought of his training. *When fighting, especially against multiple enemies, always strike first gaining the element of surprise. Also, having multiple moves, a plan. Disabled the first one and then use it as a shield against the others. At least control the first one and throw it into someone else.*

He approached Elisa, which was the young lady being intimidated. She had not backed down, getting louder against them, showing no fear.

"Hi, I am behind you, a friend, please my Lilith wants to speak with you, let me handle this." Elisa had turned around, first thinking it was someone in management but quickly realizing it was just another patron.

"Please just turn around and go to my table, I got this." Pluto pointing to the table.

Elisa was a bit confused; she turned around and started to move to the table, stopping quickly as Pluto was now facing the center man.

"You know when I woke up today, I said it is a good day to die! How about you?" Pluto asked.

He waited and looked into his eyes, like the man's answer really mattered. Just as he was about to speak, Pluto attacked.

Lilith instantly told Matt to go help him, unfortunately he hesitated, saying, "His orders were to protect you, I can't go against his orders." It was more of a plea, to forgive him as if there was nothing he could do.

Lilith never forgave him for that, in his defense once the action started, he really would not have had time to be any support other than to avenge his captain's murderers if that were the case.

When Pluto was close enough to you, he had perfected his right leg front kick. He could apply it without the victim having any chance of avoiding it. The only part of his body that moved was his right leg extremely hard and quickly towards the kneecap. Usually hitting below that area with such force to move his victim's upper body forward towards him.

Right when the man had opened his mouth, before any word or sound came out, Pluto had kicked him hard right below his right kneecap. Then with a full half turn of his body he gave him a right hook, hitting flush on the man's ear. Most would have stopped or slowed down, most were not Pluto.

He finished the fight with a left straight punch to his chest, landing a bit off the bone to the left. Then without hesitation grabbed and used him, throwing him into the other human on his left.

Pluto's attack was quick and if there were only two opponents he would have succeeded, unfortunately there were three against him. As he turned to face the non-human, a gun was pointed at him.

Then the man went down, Elisa had never gone to Pluto's table. She had pulled her gun, firing at the same moment Pluto turned to face the third enemy. She shot first, her weapon set to stun. Later it was revealed that the non-human's gun pointed at Pluto was set to kill.

Pluto had hurt the first man, with the second only being slightly bruised. Security had arrived quickly with everyone now going over the details.

Once everyone identity was figured out the mood of their security force changed. Pluto had grown a beard and mustache, both having the color of silver gray. He looked quite different than clean shaven and was not easily recognizable as Plutoneus.

The management who was now involved with their security, thanked Pluto for his brave fight in protecting the galaxy. They were sorry about the incident and there would be no charge for the meals.

Also, no actions would be taken against him concerning the altercation.

In that area all three beings apologized saying if they had known who he was it would have never happened.

The restaurant did ask very politely for Pluto and company to leave and please not to return. At that point Pluto was ready to go, still he had a request or demand, it was always hard to tell the difference between the two when dealing with him.

Also, he liked to feel in control, even when being thrown out of an establishment.

Elisa was young, with a spirit that had not been crushed by her surroundings. She was on the smaller size with the most beautiful skin color Pluto had ever seen. It was the lightest shade of brown which just picked up all the light around it, sometimes giving it a golden tone. Her black hair and perfectly proportioned body finished her outside appearance.

It was her internal spirit, her aura that interested Pluto. So many people were broken in spirit, resigning themselves to just accept things. Elisa was just the opposite, which was what attracted Pluto's attention.

Turning to Elisa he asked, "How would you like to travel with us, we are exploring the galaxy."

Her face lit up, she had a beautiful smile and answered, "Really? Yes, yes, I want to come along!"

Now looking at the official, Pluto said, "No problem as long as..." He hesitated not yet knowing her name.

"Elisa" she interjected.

Pluto continued, "Elisa comes with us. I am quite ready to leave." With a big smile now appearing on his face.

Lilith in retrospect was incredibly happy to have Elisa on board. There were no other woman for her to bond with, also she at once had a warm feeling towards her. Elisa had saved her captain which she loved unconditionally.

A VOLUNTEER

Two weeks later, Elisa had acclimated well with becoming part of the ships crew. Spending most of her time with Matt, Orlando, and Lilith. They would have their woman talks, with sometimes Lilith blushing or Elisa giggling.

Pluto had been preoccupied during that period, spending little time with his crew and even less with Elisa.

It was during their group meal that Pluto broke the news.

"I have good news; I know where Dragonfly is, and she will be there when we arrive." He stopped to check the looks he was receiving from his crew.

"Unfortunately, she is a prisoner in the toughest lockup in our galaxy. Located on the planet Pew. I only need one volunteer for an extremely dangerous mission."

At that point, Matt who had felt bad about their last outing, said firmly, "I will go with you captain!"

Pluto shaking his head slightly up and down in approval when Elisa's voice was heard.

"Please captain take me instead."

For the first time their captain hesitated with his response. That was very unusual as Pluto gave most things little thought before replying.

As he was thinking, Lilith made her thoughts known.

"Why are you doing this, just for some weapons you want? That can not be that important that you are willing to risk not only your life but also others." The room was silent, that was the first time anyone ever heard Lilith complain, and no less about what their captain wanted to do.

Pluto looked solemn, "You are right, I would never do this just for the weapons. People act like I had done something great; they are so wrong. I did not save the galaxy; all I did was cost eight million brave souls to perish and I to be captured. One person solely saved our galaxy…Dragonfly! She saved you, my dearest Lilith and everyone else. I owe it to her to help her gain freedom."

The Pilot broke the deafening silence that had filled the room.

"Captain, I was there at the Final Battle, far away from the main field, when I saw the green glow, I tried to get there but by the time I did, you were all gone. I have held that guilt for too long now, I will go with you."

Pluto trying to ease the atmosphere replied, "Soon everyone will want to go." Finishing with a smile. Then resuming his more serious approach started to speak again."

"Thank you, my friend, please you have only my utmost respect. Thank you for your service, only you know how bad it was. I am sorry I did not remember you. For my plan to work, and the odds are well against it, I need someone young. I appreciate your offer, but you have an extremely important function here on this ship while the plan is in progress."

They were all waiting to see who he would pick; Lilith still was upset waiting till they went to bed before discussing it more.

"Thank you, Matt, for volunteering, this time Elisa will help me." Pluto now was all business in speech and manner.

"Yes!" Elisa shouted with Pluto giving her the strangest look, it had a sadness about it. The look when an older person knows what youth has yet to learn.

Pluto continued to explain his plan, it involved the pilot, Elisa, and him. As he finished, seeing the looks on the rest of his crew, especially Lilith, with her disapproving stare.

"Well, lets all sleep on it, two jumps will be needed before we are close. Elisa you can still change your mind." Pluto making the discussion over, except for tonight with Lilith.

The pilot became Matt and Orlando prime target, once the captain had left with Lilith, the questions began. The survivors, which were very few, never wanted to talk about it.

"How many First People did you kill?" Questions of that nature plus trying to find out more what their captain did, came from both younger men.

His replied was the same to both on each question, "I don't want to talk about it."

Finally, he said, "Being in a battle like that, changes you, it is not how many you killed, your thoughts are more on all those you lost, some saving you while they died. We tried but like the captain said, we lost. I will not say another word on this subject, and I strongly suggest not to ask again!"

Lilith looking at the man she loved, trying to support his passions yet at what point?

"Does my love not mean anything? You are so ready to risk everything, all the time, do you not care about dying and leaving me to dwell in misery without you?" Lilith asked.

"My dearest Lilith, your love is everything to me, it is just Dragonfly deserves better."

"Then let someone else help, contact people, why do you have to do it?"

"Dragonfly gave me the gift of extended life; without her weapons I would have died in the Final Battle. After this, lets settled down, pick any planet you like, hopefully with less gravity than Earth!" Now Pluto was smiling at his beloved.

Opening up his arms and feeling her come into his embrace. When you are hugging someone, you love the most, it is impossible not to comply with their wishes.

"My sweet, wonderful Lilith, I promise this is the last mission, then it will be just you and me, until you get tired of me." Now with a huge smile Pluto looking into her eyes.

Lilith hated that he was doing it while loving his sense of loyalty and admiring his courage. These were some of the reasons she loved him so much. She was learning that love is always standing with your partner, even if they are headed into quicksand.

If he did survive this challenge what she really wanted was waiting for them. Knowing he would not break his promise, she only had to worry one more time.

NATHAN

People on the ship now were different, each thinking about what was to come. Most feeling guilty they were not doing more. Of course, it was not their fault, following orders, even when the orders are to do nothing, can be the hardest to follow.

Matt and Orlando pleaded with the captain to also take them beside Elisa. If not both then at least one of them.

The captain reply was, "The plan will work best having just one other besides myself." His mood had changed now, like a fighter getting ready for battle. It is a mindset, extreme focus only on one thing. There were no more smiles or jokes, their captain war face was on.

Elisa persona also had changed, she was going into the fire, each person handles that type of pressure differently. She seemed like the captain now, all business.

Matt had caught the captain alone and asked, "Can I speak freely?"

Pluto giving him a long look, "Sure Matt, what is on your mind?"

"Captain, how do you know you can trust Elisa, she is not really one of us. I am sorry about the lunch incident on the planet." Matt finished speaking but still was not done.

Pluto jumping in right after he finished his last sentence, "Nothing to be sorry about, your orders were to protect Lilith. Trust me, if you broke those orders we would be having a vastly different conversation. Elisa protected me at her own risk, she is now part of our crew and one of us! Truth, there is a great chance that neither of us will make it back. Let just say you are right, and I cannot trust Elisa, who do you think I want on this ship protecting my Lilith? Your orders are to always protect Lilith at all costs."

Matt replied, "I will, captain." Then after Pluto left, Matt thought how smart his commander was, how much he could learn from that man. He still wanted to go yet now understood the reasons of why he had to remain.

Pluto before the mission had a private conversation with Elisa.

Near the end he said, "So you understand what must be done, you are a key part to the plan's success. Are you sure you can do it?"

Elisa's eyes never left his, "Trust me captain, I will not let you down."

———

The planet Pew was small, just a little larger than Earth's moon. Having only one building on its surface, the rest lying underground. Considered the only inescapable prison in the galaxy, its unfortunate tenants thought to be extremely dangerous but for whatever reasons still needed to be kept alive.

Pew's sun was farther away then Earth's moon was from its sun giving it always a gloomy appearance. Having a thick cloud layer to finish its unappealing atmosphere.

Rocks were the main attraction on the surface, with the lack of sunlight and the poor soil truly little plant life existed.

There was one building not exceptionally large that broke thru. Its function was to transfer the new prisoners to the prison, which was far below the surface. The process involved three elevators, each separated by circular walkways.

Some prisons are built not just to keep people within but also keeping all others out. Breaking into Pew's prison was as hard as trying to escape.

One man had complete control within its walls, power like that makes anyone evil. Nathan was a big man, having long hair and a beard plus mustache, resembling a mountain man that lived on Earth. Still being young and having great power plus a very smart mind, he enjoyed his position controlling all things.

His voice was on the higher end, which contradicted his look, yet he moved around the facility with speed, showing up when least expected on his guards. He used what resembled a tablet that was attached to his arm. It was translucent and very sturdy.

Often, he would check it, as it watched all the areas and functions of the prison. Having its own space and land defense, which both would need to be breach before trying to gain access to the elevators.

Each ride down the shafts, which were the nickname for the elevators, had its own security force separated from the others. Once in the prison, the lowest section reserved for their worst beings. With the entire compound not having any windows while providing the barest necessities of life, made anyone living there depressed, including the guards.

Most of the prison security force only stay there for five years, it found longer stays caused emotional problems. They had better living conditions yet it did not really help much.

To Nathan it was paradise, he was never depressed being there. His accommodations were much better than what everyone else had. And of course, they should be, were his thoughts. How he got Dragonfly was purely by luck, and the actual taking her there he had nothing to do with.

Yet to hear how he bragged about being her master, you would think he had done something. Truth is once you are in the hole, which was the common name used by all there, you are never getting out.

Even with the greatness of Dragonfly's intelligence, without a huge assault and even with that, there still was an incredible low chance of escape. As the slogan goes inside the prison, once in, never out, nothing but the hole.

Nathan liked to verbally insult Dragonfly; she was defying him by not speaking to anyone, especially him.

As he stood in front of her contaminant cell, which was at the very bottom level of the complex, he began.

"I have researched your history; you are supposed to be so smart and yet, here you are, in the hole, never to leave! I will make you a deal if you speak to me. How would you like an extra hour of light?" Now having his big smile and laughing at her. Nathan was extremely strict when it came to her. Dragonfly was only given nine hours of light with the rest in complete darkness.

She looked at him, with a slight grin and said nothing. That simple act infuriated Nathan more than anything she might have spoken.

She was his prisoner and eventually would submit to his authority. He wanted to break her spirit, but she was strong in that area. His mind raged with evil thoughts, finally giving him kudos for being her master.

"You will die here, I will always be your master, think about that!" And then Nathan moved on leaving Dragonfly to a hell she did not deserve.

Pew was created by the Core and other large conglomerates that controlled the galaxy. They wanted a place to put people that truly interfered with their businesses. Collectively they funded it and chose its commandant to run it. There was never a lack of funds or resources for its needs.

Because of its backers and there being no one really in charge of their galaxy, it existed but was not talked about.

Nathan was born to a wealthy family and was fascinated with Pew since childhood. He made it his life's obsession to become its commandant. His intelligence was clear from his youth, that with his focus on one goal, plus his families' connections, was granted his command.

He was perfect for their needs in running the prison. Most hated working there, never wanting to devote their lives to its management. Except for Nathan, even the guards had fears that one day they would be in one of its cells.

Dragonfly was one of its prisoners but not because she had done anything wrong. Nathan had obsessions in capturing and imprisoning certain people. To that end he had a special extraction force working on a list of people he wanted.

She had made that list since it was known that she was extremely smart. Capturing and detaining someone like that made Nathan felt he was smarter than her. The longer he held her, especially for no real reason, just made it that much better.

The fallacy that if someone were extremely smart that they could not be captured or tricked is wrong. Everyone makes mistakes or has weak moments when others might take advantage of them.

Also, the fact that the extraction team was highly trained on doing just one function, kidnapping people, made them an extremely dangerous force.

Daily, he insulted and tried to set up a dialogue with Dragonfly. At one point even physically tortured her, all to no avail. Now just verbally insulting her was good enough.

There was one room there that was beautiful, it was created with the intentions of forgetting where it was located. The ceiling was over fifty feet high, with holographic images of clouds, sunlight, varied color skies. That with its huge size plus walls that also had monitors displaying large windows with many diverse types of scenes shown.

Once inside it was easy to forget where it was, in a terrible prison. The mind can quickly saturate itself with sights, sounds and gentle breezes, making it forget the real reality it occupies.

Nathan had returned to his paradise to refresh his spirit, even to him being outside his room too long, worked on the sanity of his mind. His peace disturbed by the sound of his watch issuing a text for direction.

All the prisoners were given numbers with their names never being used once in the hole.

A guard began, "Commandant, 31862407 somehow got a pencil and was writing on the floor under his bed, what would you like done?"

He could have said, removed the pencil, or give him some paper or make him clean up the writing under the bed. What he said was the following.

"Get the pencil and put 31862407 into isolation, indefinitely."

"Yes Commandant." Thinking to himself, *the only thing worse than being here is isolation. That man has no heart.*

The complex had an impressive space defense, which was completely automated. Once activated no other actions were required.

THE GREAT RESCUE

Pluto was having private meetings with each person on his ship. Going over instructions about the plan, or the Great Rescue as it now was called. Pluto gave that name to the mission at hand. It sounded noble and right to do, he always knew the value of words.

Regardless of the name, Lilith was not happy, and no pleasant words would change that. Alone in their room with her captain, to her he was so much more than that. She had seen sides of his personality that few others knew.

He had given her life and had put himself at risk in doing it. Getting injured without complaint, that was just who he was. She hated that he would risk it all for Dragonfly. Lilith was a very smart person; she understood her love for Pluto had to exist without changing him.

She was researching planets for their new life once this mission was over. Trying to focus only on the future and not their current situation. Finding a perfect planet that had lower gravity plus higher oxygen content levels than Earth. With the sale of their ship, they would have plenty of funds for their future life together.

Everyone had a different thought on what was going to happen. Like they each had a different version of what was coming. Lilith tried to find out, but each crew member said they had sworn to secrecy on providing any details.

Even Elisa, who was Lilith's closest friend on the ship, was silent in that area, revealing almost nothing of what the captain had said to her.

All were tense except Pluto, having a very nonchalant attitude about the Great Rescue. Even though it was only Elisa and Pluto taking the risks, all were affected by it. Matt watched Lilith whenever in his sight. The pilot also seemed troubled, like he knew something important and holding it in was making him ill.

When Lilith addressed those things to Pluto he replied, "Just nerves flaring up, typical before a big mission." Acting as if it all were normal, yet what he was trying to do, was as far as normal can become.

They were still far away but in space terms would be there soon. They had jump far from where Pew was located. Now traveling at a high rate of speed yet still having a large distance to go. In five hours, it would all begin.

Lilith had stopped talking to Pluto, and the rest of the crew. Making it noticeably clear she did not approve of what was happening and those who were making it possible. She felt that his power, their captain over his crew was unreal. They would do or not do whatever he asked.

She loved him yet still would question his actions or thoughts. She wondered how that power felt, there was so many things she had not experienced. Laughing at her prior self, just a brain stuck without the senses that make living worth living.

For the first time she felt bad for the other AI stuck in life on a motherboard. Pluto knew there were others yet cared nothing about them. Many times, asking herself why he had helped her. Now she knew what being truly conflicted was, again laughing to herself. Her thoughts, *life is so wonderful and painful, at times in the same moment.*

Elisa was the most out of character from the others, which was understandable on what she was facing. Her silence and frozen face, which now showed no happiness or sadness. Just a cold stare of someone that was ready for the unknown.

Pluto who either was truly relaxed or just trying to ease the tension his crew were feeling, was all smiles. There appeared no worries about the Great Rescue that were upon him. More than that, he was happier than ever before, with a big smile shown to all.

Lilith thought to herself, *the plan if you could call it that, was more like a hope wrapped in a wish and sent with a prayer.*

Deciding to have a private conversation with the pilot, Lilith went to the flight deck, luckily, he was alone.

Looking in his eyes, "Don, how can he be so calm? He is betting his life on a hope that what he thinks will happen, will actually happen. What if he is wrong, everything will be lost."

The pilot was old, waiting a moment or two before responding.

"He is used to it, he fought the Core for ten years, many times in positions just like this. Once the Final Battle started it was obvious we were going to lose, the First People were the greatest fighters ever seen. He fought with us, surviving all they could dish out. Did you see the video of him and the fighters on their last charge? Then surviving and coming back, I imagine to him, this really is not that big a deal."

Lilith looked at him, not understanding how humans can so quickly put their existence on the line. Now that she was human, death never was too far away in her mind. She also realized that there still was much more to know about her Pluto, she had done a search on his records but now realized it was not complete.

There were only a few hours left before they would begin the mission. Lilith wanted to talk with Pluto before it began.

"You promise this is the last mission, then you retire? I have found the perfect planet, low gravity, and high oxygen." Lilith paused there to smile at her beloved.

Pluto responded with one word and open arms, "Yes." Now waiting for his love to enter his space. Lilith closed the gap and gave him a wonderful hug, fully pressed into his body he could feel her heartbeat and her lungs breathing. They stayed embraced for quite some time, neither wanting to break the moment.

The intercom killing the silence like thunder, "Captain we are within range and ready when you are."

11

THE HOLE

Not much changed on a day-to-day basis inside the hole, time disappeared. Nathan lived a somewhat normal life, compliments of his wonderful rooms. Yet for everyone else, just routine happened.

That also was a result of Nathan, he wanted everything to run like clockwork. The guards would have to check in to perform their normal functions, all watched by cameras. If that was not enough, they had to deal with Nathan who lately had become more eccentric in his actions.

Working in a place like that takes it toll not only on the prisoners but the guards too. Very few stayed past their five-year contract, especially with a huge payday waiting to spend.

Ben was old and still had the lowest guard ranking, he could leave anytime he wanted. Talk was he had been there for over ten years. Hating authority and being cynical in his last years, he was outspoken about his thoughts on the hole.

He was in the monitoring center when the shuttle that was damaged, crashed into Pew.

Speaking to the others in the room while not really to anyone of them, "She is coming in hot; I will contact Nathan about it."

Most hated communicating with Nathan, he had an arrogant attitude.

Ben contacted Nathan and said, "Commandant, we have a ship that just crash landed up there."

Nathan was on a video connection, "So why are you telling me this?"

"I want to do a recon and need your permission to go to the surface."

Nathan replied, "Yes you do, not just my permission but my commands to each level to allow you to pass. Create a broadcast and take someone with you."

———

As they were getting ready to begin the rescue of Dragonfly, Pluto whispered into the pilot ear, "Don, don't hold back, make it believable."

Then he and Elisa entered the shuttle, she sat in the pilot chair and were ready to go, Pluto stopped her.

"Handcuff me now and don't forget the tape!" Pluto using his captain's authority, which was hard to disobey.

Elisa answered, "Yes captain." She started to handcuff his hands in front of his body with Pluto stopping her again.

"In the back, its all about being believable." Now there was a touch of anger in his voice.

She unlocked the restraints and reapplied them now with his hands behind his back. Elisa was going to suggest she tape his mouth once they arrived yet now just obeyed his orders.

Elisa had never driven a shuttle after it has been fired upon, she thought that *life is about firsts. This will add to that list,* yet the truth, she was scared. Keeping a brave face for the captain was easier to do, then shutting out the thoughts within her head.

Pluto handcuffed with his hands behind his back and his mouth taped shut. They were moving as fast as the shuttle could, heading towards Pew. It is a weird feeling knowing that very shortly you would be crashing into a planet.

Hopefully, the planet's space defense was not on, and they would be alive after the hit. Those thoughts and much more were in Elisa mind. The last thing her captain told her was to try and relaxed as much as she can, it will help her handle the impact of the crash.

She looked at him, his breathing was calm and there was no fear in his eyes. Thinking, in some ways he was amazing. Maybe he just did not care about life, yet she knew that was not true.

At that moment everything changed, the cabin pressure had blown out thru the broken windows. There were fires in multiple places, and it felt like her skin had burned on her face and hands.

The sounds became deafening as the planet's atmosphere was thrusting in. Controls were unresponsive as she watched the ground rapidly approaching. She was able to level the ship out, giving them a chance of survival.

Elisa never expected the pilot, Don, to fire a shot that powerful and to hit the engines, both causing major trouble for Pluto and herself.

They hit hard, so hard Elisa chair dislodged from the floor throwing Elisa and the chair into the side wall. She now had a bad cut on her face, which was bleeding profusely while also having a broken nose and arm. The good news she was not spitting out blood, so there were no internal injuries.

No matter what name he used there was one thing always consistent with Pluto, his luck. His chair did not break away and there was truly little redness on his face and hands. Thinking to himself how he had survived so many crashes and yet walked away with no real injuries.

There were no sounds now except for the howl of the wind and Elisa moaning. She was in bad shape; the blood was slowing down that leaked from her face. Having hit her head hard, now having a slight concussion plus more pain in her arm.

Pluto not moving or doing anything, just waited.

———

As soon as Don had fired on the shuttle, he set a new course and made the jump in space. It was a short jump and fifteen minutes later they were at their new destination. The galaxy had communication hubs; situated around in key spots to broadcast crucial information.

Don now had assumed the captain's role; he sent the message he wanted broadcasts. Figuring it would get rejected, knowing he would need to go up the ladder to find the person with the right powers to make it happen.

After thirty minutes of arguing and waiting finally the director of that station was on the line.

Don started again, he already had a list of names and numbers, "Sir, please your name and title?" After that was transmitted and spoken Don said the following.

"This is not a joke, that message needs to be sent out now!"

"How can I know this is real?" Was the response from the director.

Don getting really upset, "If you don't do it now, I will let everyone know your lack of actions, killed him! I was at the Final Battle, I answered the call, I am telling you it is Plutoneus. I personally will kill you, if not done now!"

There was a moment of silence as the two men were looking at each other via the monitor's screens.

Then the man responded with, "My sister was there, she only sent one message during her time, that she was so proud of everyone there. Plutoneus, she said fought beside her and her team. That there would never be anything more important that she would do, then compared to what she was doing. I will send the message, but hear me clearly, I know who you are, if you're lying, I will kill you!"

He ended with, "I will see you there."

Don nodded his head and then turned to the remaining members of the crew.

"Lilith, please go with Matt to the planet below."

Matt who looked sad moved towards Lilith to escort her to another shuttle.

Lilith looking at them all, "I will go with you."

For the first time Don's voice became lower when addressing her with, "No, this may be a one-way trip, and I cannot break those orders from the captain. We are not coming back without him!"

Lilith turned to Matt, "You want to go with them, don't you?"

Matt looking somber, "Yes, but I promised the captain I will protect you, can't break his orders."

She thought to herself, they all are willing to die for him, I love him but do not want to die. Am I truly human to love someone so much yet still want to live. She wanted to know why they felt so strongly and why she never would willingly die for someone else.

She looked at the men standing in front of her, "God's speed." And turned to Matt with a look that said let's go.

DOWNWARD

Ben and another guard got into the hover craft and without making any sound it started moving amazingly fast to the target destination, one crashed shuttle. When they arrived, there were small fires and smoke that could easily be seen from the outside. The shell was mostly intact with its side ripped open.

The other guard just enjoyed being outside the hole, it was a rare pleasure for any inside.

"Are you okay? Do you know where you are?" Ben asked as he approached the ship. He could see there were two occupants, one was a prisoner of the other having his mouth tapped shut.

The young girl looked hurt, having a face wound and was dealing with a semi concussion. They formed an odd scene, begging for an explanation.

Again, he repeated, "Are you okay, what happened and who is your prisoner?" Now moving closer to Elisa.

The crash had really hurt her head, just getting thoughts together was a struggle.

"Kinda okay, I have a claim filed with the Core." At that she stopped talking.

Ben realized the claim was for her prisoner and that she needed medical attention.

"Well come with us and we will fix you up, process your claim and secure the prisoner."

He waited a few minutes, realizing her mind was trying to process what he had just said. Most would have been impatient, just being out of the hole was worth waiting on her slow response.

"Okay" was all she said, they help her to the hover craft showing no concern for her prisoner's health or chance of escape. There really was none unless another shuttle craft landed and rescued him.

After Elisa had been help into her seat and provided water, they then retrieved Pluto. The difference in how they treated him was clear, they had a disdain for all prisoners, he was roughly picked up, pulled, and pushed towards their vehicle.

As they were riding back to the entrance of the hole, Ben asked, "Why did you tape his mouth shut, did he talk to much?" He was smiling as he said it.

"He is dangerous, best not to listen to anything he says." Elisa answering, now her mind thinking better than before.

Their trip was short given the speed of the craft but getting into the hole was as hard as getting out. The first checkpoint was the door at the surface, the start of three elevator rides down to the prison.

The guards at each level had been contacted by Nathan with the instructions to let them in, process, and bring them to the lowest level.

Before they went down on the first elevator ride, Elisa's prisoner had all his clothes and possessions removed, Pluto had brought nothing with him. Then they performed an identification check, issued new clothes and to them the most important thing, his number.

The guards informed Elisa it was a crime to refer to any prisoner by name, their number was the only way to address them. They removed her weapons and allowed her to continue.

They then applied new handcuffs and leg chains to prisoner 224766620, and all followed the circular path to the next elevator.

Once started it descended quickly and for over five minutes. No one had spoken yet the feeling of now being in a prison and never getting out, started forming in Elisa's mind. Finally, the elevator stopped when the new floor appeared, looking like the one they had just left.

As they descended downwards it reflected the mood and atmosphere of the people there. Depressing is just a word, Pew's prison gave it form, making it a true piece of reality. You could feel it in the walls, ceilings, and floors. Every fixture spoke it.

The lighting gave off a yellowish glow, everything whether alive or dead gave the impression that they hated to be there.

This aspect of their mission never entered Elisa's mind. So many what if thoughts, with no nice answers to any of them. She watched Pluto, he seemed unaffected by everything around him. They had removed the tape over his mouth, yet he never uttered a single word.

Pluto was thinking that stage one of his plan was working, it was the easy part. Now the real question was if stage two will succeed or even happen?

They reached the next level and then identified themselves to the guards. It went much quicker than the level before and within fifteen minutes they were on the second elevator heading to the third elevator which then led to the the prison.

Upon arrival at the third elevator, they again named themselves to the guards on that level. The procedure was identical to what they had just been thru. In the third elevator it felt more finale. They had traveled so far down into the planet, further into any planet then Elisa or Pluto had ever traveled.

The feeling that they would never see the surface again became an obsession on Elisa's brain. Never experiencing that type of fear before, all her thoughts were to run away. To get out of this unnatural and ominous structure.

They then were brought to Nathan per his orders, it was a long walk going down four flights of stairs until they reached the lowest level of the prison.

Nathan was extremely pleased with himself, not only did he have the smartest person, but he now also had the most dangerous. Of course, he did not believe that Dragonfly was the smartest or Plutoneus the most dangerous.

He was having delusions that if he had them both, then he was the smartest, most dangerous person period. As a collector, he could not have chosen two greater archetypes.

He like talking to Dragonfly daily and had gotten used to only hearing his own voice, so when she replied that day, it startled him.

The group came into the room with Pluto handcuffed, two guards in front and two behind him. They never took chances when prisoners were not in their cells.

Nathan who had been teasing Dragonfly on how she still was his prisoner, being in mid sentence as they appeared before him.

Now putting his full attention to his new prisoner. Looking on his monitor attached to his left arm, he began.

Prisoner 224766620, I am going to make an exception with you for today, so enjoy it. It will be the last time your name will ever be heard.

Then looking at Dragonfly said, "So this is the great Plutoneus that has come to rescue you. The great warrior was how they spoke about him. What I see, is just an old weak man, someone who never was what they said."

For the first time she responded back, "Nathan, you have invited your doom into your home, he will destroy you, this prison and most of the guards and inmates." Now she was smiling, laughing like it was the funniest thing she had ever seen.

Dragonfly continued, "He fought the Core for ten years and they could not kill him, then he went to Antarctica and destroyed the First People's base. He went to Mars and the planet was attacked and almost destroyed, all because of him. He fought General Max and not only still lived but killed the general. He led the Final Battle and was taken by the First People and yet he still lives. The First People were smart enough to get rid of him, sending him as far away from their society as possible. Don't you realize how dangerous he is?"

Nathan was not impressed, "You are supposed to be so smart, yet you speak nonsense. Do you not see what I see, he it toothless, old, weak, and most importantly my prisoner. He has no power, and I will prove it to you."

He pulled out his gun and shot Elisa, she went down like all dead people do, hitting the floor hard. He then looked at the monitor on his arm, asking if the Core's battleship had arrived.

The response was not what he expected.

"Yes Commandant, but they are not responding to our communications. They are just sitting out there, waiting."

Dragonfly excitedly said the following, "Nathan, he will kill you for that, you need to kill him now!"

Shouting at her, "I am in total control, heck I don't even think he is awake. He shows no care about her or himself for that matter."

Looking at Pluto he asked, "So do you care about her, are you going to kill me?"

Pluto just stared at him, which made Nathan even more upset.

"Are you going to be like her? Giving me the silent treatment, and 5469942, I like you better when you did not talk."

Now the board on his arm came alive, "Commandant, there are 8 ships in our space zone. More are coming, the space defenses are on, what else do you want done.?"

As Nathan was assessing the situation, the numbers on his monitor went from eight to twenty-three ships above the planet.

His guards were concerned about all the ships above, their defenses were strong and could handle that number of ships, yet if more came without reinforcements they would be in trouble.

Nathan responded to his guards, "We can handle five times that number of ships. Try to contact the Core's battleship again. Also, contact the Core directly and our other friends and request help."

Dragonfly was laughing and shaking her head, "You are making all the wrong decisions, if you do not want to kill him, be like the First People who are incredibly wise and send him away from here. Give him a shuttle and take him to the surface before it is too late."

Nathan thinking this is the first time he ever saw Dragonfly scared. She has been locked in the most secure prison in the galaxy and showed no concern. Now she was afraid and wanted her rescuer killed. It made no sense to him; his communicator went off with the message that followed.

"Commandant, there are now over two hundred and seventy ships, and more are showing up every second. The Core battleship has left, and no one is responding to our request for help. They are not even willing to talk to us. Sir we are now receiving a message from the force above."

Nathan for the first time started to realize the gravity of his situation. Like a shock to the system, it felt unbelievable that just taking one man into his prison could cause such problems.

"What did they say?" Nathan asked, which was an unusual experience for him.

The guard responded with, "They said return the great Plutoneus unharmed within ten minutes or they will destroy our air defense and then begin a ground assault ending with the death of everyone inside."

Then the guard added, "Sir, there are now over five hundred ships and more are coming. We must give up the prison, please Commandant, there are just too many of them!"

Nathan was now having trouble thinking, he did not like to be rushed. He was so used to setting time constrains for others, never for himself. Still trying to understand how everything could fall apart so quickly. He was fighting his reality instead of accepting it and figuring out a new plan.

The guards were all now starting to panic, which was clear even with the guards around them.

Nathan last communication from the guards above were, "Sir we are leaving, surrendering and going to a safe place on the surface."

A sound was then heard that stopped everyone.

"Hold on, setup a broadcast from here to the ships above, this is Plutoneus, and I am commanding you to obey my orders."

It was the first time they had heard him speak; it was with authority, sounding legendary. Making the guards do as he had demanded. All things were changing so quickly with Plutoneus now in control.

Then he motioned the guard to remove his restraints and looking into the camera began.

"This is Plutoneus, thank you all for coming, I will never ask again. I will give Nathan the commandant a chance and want you all to see it."

Then he turned to Nathan and said, "Nathan, I will give you a sporting chance, here are my terms, let me know if you accept them. We will fight right now, either hand to hand or sword to sword. If you win, you will release all the prisoners. You, the guards, and prisoners will go to the surface, and they will take you to safety. Then this prison will be destroyed! I want nothing left of it. If I win, the same conditions apply except Nathan, you will not be joining us. Do you agree?"

Poor Nathan was still trying to understand that the prison was lost, it just was unbelievable to him. Then he replayed in his mind what Plutoneus said and started to smile.

"Either way I lose my prison, that does not feel right."

Plutoneus getting annoyed reply, "You get to live, that does not feel right to me! Do you accept, yes or no."

"I accept and choose swords, obviously you do not know, I am an expert swordsman. I have studied many diverse types and have a pair of Japanese Samurai swords from your planet Earth." Nathan now motioned a guard to get them. As they were waiting Plutoneus went to a guard and asked for his knife. It had a fifteen-inch blade and reminded him of a Roman short sword, just a bit smaller than that.

When the swords were brought into the room, Plutoneus spoke.

"Nathan I would rather use this knife against your sword, do you have any objections?"

Now a huge smile appeared on Nathan's face, knowing his sword was more than three times the length of that knife. Starting to feel at least good in the thought of killing Plutoneus, he asked Dragonfly the following question.

"Why would he do that, just plain stupid!"

Dragonfly responded, "He wants to be close to you when he kills you. To look into your dying eyes while feeling your last breath."

There was quite a different feeling now in the room, regardless of this fight most would live, all their attention now going to the two warriors' moments before their battle.

Nathan was doing practice swings, and it was quite apparent his skill in using that weapon. The sword was long having a slight arc to it shape. Its blade was razor sharp and its construction showed the love of its creator.

Everyone was watching the event, from all the people on the ships above the surface to all the guards in the prison. The event was also being streamed to many locations within the galaxy.

Plutoneus was in a meditation state. He had slowed down his breathing, his eyes were open but appeared not to focus on anything in front of him. They would periodically close and then open. It almost appeared he was on the verge of falling asleep. The guards were making bets on who would be victorious. The favorite obviously was Nathan, between his skill and weapon's size advantage it did not appear it would last long.

There was an accessible area that did have a few obstructions but was the only space available at their current location.

The men approached from either side of that space, now there was not a sound in the room. There was an intensity to each man, Nathan was young, big, and in his prime. Holding a most beautiful weapon that was made just for this type of fight. His power and focus permeated his being.

On the other side was an old man, standing calmly without making any movements. It appeared he was not even breathing; he was that calm. Pluto held his knife which was a nice weapon but no match for what it was going against. He had it close to the middle of his body. His eyes almost appeared not to blink as he was now within striking distance of Nathan, who was moving slowly at him.

First, he tested his nerves, making wide swinging motion with his sword but not yet looking to strike, testing Plutoneus if he would take any actions. The old man just stood there, not blinking, watching and ready yet doing nothing.

Quickly Nathan changed the trajectory and if not blocked would have caused serious injuries. At the last second Plutoneus moved his knife to block the strike and rolled his body towards Nathan, traveling inwards after the block.

That action pushed Nathan back as his sword was much more effective while Plutoneus was farther away. They played that scene a couple of times. Nathan still a bit too close for a good strike, taking one anyhow with Plutoneus luckily blocking and moving forward to shorten the distance between them.

It was odd to see, the young man with the big sword be pushed back by an old man with a little knife.

Unfortunately, that did not last long, with Nathan calming down and starting a different approach, which worked much better. Instead of going for one killer stroke, he started making cuts on Plutoneus' body. First one was below his shoulder on his upper arm, then the lower leg on his left side.

Nathan now had full control and was just toying with him, at this point able to kill him whenever he chose.

Plutoneus started to change color, his blood seeping out and spreading to all the areas not changed yet. It became a sad sight to see, with most wishing Nathan would just end it already.

Nathan was having fun, there are few things as exciting as fighting for your life and winning. He had never experienced anything that intense. Finally, he was ready, and Plutoneus also was.

He started to approach Nathan in an unusual way then before. His right arm was extended and hanging low, down near his upper leg. His left arm was just the opposite, away from his body above his head. It looked like a bear hug on an angle.

Now Nathan saw exactly what he wanted to do. With an amazing fast and exact swing, as he turned his hips and followed thru cutting Plutoneus's arm off right at the elbow. Everyone was looking at the arm and hand laying there on the floor.

It looked surreal, like a movie prop just lying there.

Nathan kept looking at that arm, yet something was wrong, there was something missing. His mind just could not put a name to it. Then he felt a slight drop of liquid running down his collarbone. Using his left hand and turning his head slightly inward towards his body, now the liquid forming a steam of blood. At that moment he realized the knife was missing from that arm and hand lying on the floor. It was in his neck, the shock now taking over his body.

Plutoneus was standing close to him, he had tossed his knife from his right hand to his left hand. A move that usually would fail ninth-nine times out of one hundred. Then while Nathan was cutting off his arm, he planted the knife deep into Nathan's neck. His adrenaline was so strong and excitement on finishing Plutoneus he never felt it.

The men were looking into each other' eyes, Nathan now dropping the sword from his right hand and sinking to the floor.

Plutoneus followed his actions, his gaze was still on him.

Then he said the following, "You did good, die with honor." With that he pulled the knife out of his neck, the blood now gushing out.

After doing that he leaned in and whisper into Nathan's ear, "We all have a final battle, each of us will lose."

A few seconds later he was helped by the guards, who put an orange paste that cover his new stump that used to be an arm. It instantly stopped the bleeding and provided pain relief. Then an organized rush began to get everyone out of the prison. The guards helping to release their prisoners. All there had enough of that place and the feeling was the quicker on the surface the better.

BIG CHANGES

Dragonfly went with Pluto as her ship was far away, also she promised to fit a robotic arm, that looked almost human, having a skin like outer layer. Pluto retrieved Elisa body to find a proper place to bury her.

Before his stay with the First People, he would have felt guilty. Pluto's thoughts about her passing still made him feel bad, just not the guilt part. *There were many decisions she made that brought her to death's door.*

He would miss her; she would reside in his memories like all the others who lived within his mind.

When he arrived back on his ship, his crew were all there waiting for his commands. After their warm greetings, they were cheering his return.

Don was the first to speak, "Cap, I never thought so many would come, heck they are still showing up! When you sent a distress call to the galaxy, the galaxy answered."

Pluto looking at his old pilot, knowing it was not as easy as his plans had made it to be.

"Don, the whole plan counted on getting that message out, without that, all would have been lost. You are the real hero today."

Dragonfly gave the coordinates to her ship, once there and after she had fitted Pluto with the latest robotic arm and hand, they had the following conversation.

"I know about your Lilith, and I have some gifts for her, well for you both." With that said she went to a table nearby and pulled out two boxes from its draw.

They held a necklace with pedant and a ring, both beautifully designed and crafted. The necklace was in gold, and wider than what was needed to hold the pedant, which consisted of a sapphire crystal. Dragonfly explained it was a body shield that will never run out of power. The power was in the crystal and the technology for the shield in the necklace.

The other box held a ring, having a pink diamond sitting on green chips that looked like grass all held together with its gold shell.

"The necklace will protect her, and the ring celebrates your soon to be marriage." Dragonfly now having a big smile on her face.

Pluto playfully asking, "So where is my necklace?" And wondering *how did she know he was going to propose?*

Dragonfly looking sad replied, "You cannot be killed, after we are all gone, dead and buried, you will still live a long time after that. Finally, you will die of old age, an extraordinarily long time from now. I thought the elixir of extended life was a gift, sorry."

Pluto mood instantly changed, realizing that all he loves will be gone and all that will be left are memories.

They traveled back to where Lilith and Matt were located and transmitted the signal for them to return to the ship.

As soon as they walked onto the ship, Pluto ran to his Lilith. He hugged her tightly and spoke the following words.

"My dearest Lilith." Now he went down on one knee and continued, "Would you honor me and become my wife?"

The crew was all there, everyone silent and waiting for her reply. Pluto was like every man who had asked a woman's hand in marriage. There is that moment when you have doubt that she will say yes. It may be for a split second or however long it takes her to respond. The fear of what if she says no.

As everyone waited for her answer, each second became an eternity.

Lilith looking at her first suitor, there was Pluto on his knee looking at her no differently than if he was a young man asking his first love for marriage. She loved him and had been waiting and dreaming they would be husband and wife.

Thinking about how silly yet important certain titles can be. She had not even looked at the ring, it would not have mattered what it was like, having no meaning in her decision. She lowered down and with her arms touching his and started to rise. Pluto followed her lead and then they were standing looking eye to eye as she replied.

"Whether today, yesterday, or tomorrow, my answer will always be yes!"

Pluto gave his Lilith a kiss on the lips that made the younger people in his crew, turn their heads. Don and the engineer having big grins without missing a thing. Then after a big, long hug, and a meal that felt like a feast, Pluto had more news for his crew.

"Lilith and I have decided to settle down and I will be selling this ship, giving each of you a very generous severance package." Then there were cheers and jeers from his crew.

Pluto continued, "We both want to thank you for your service, care and being the type of people you are. My life is going to be much different, so if you get into trouble...don't call me!"

Now he was smiling with Lilith joining him, both smiling standing there, one arm wrapped around the other.

The end.

12

EPILOGUE

Twenty years later, she sat daydreaming, thinking about the past, present, and future. Most felt unreal, like pleasant dreams that belie reality' presence. She had changed so much both physically, mentality and emotionally, to the point that her past was more like a vague memory.

Now a mother of the most wonderful young lady, at only fourteen years old it was obvious her abilities in math plus her wit, she would achieve much.

Blanche, Lilith only daughter gave her life the greatest meaning she could imagine. She remembered Pluto saying how the greatest love is creating another being. When she thought of him, a smile always appeared.

Now he was calling himself, Barnabas, when she asked him why he chose that name, she already knew but liked hearing him describe such things. He responded it was from a TV show called, Dark Shadows, who's main character was a monster trying to pretend he was human.

Wondering how many more names he would acquire before his time was up. In that regard, he had barely aged two years during their time together. Thinking that he will outlive her brought comfort. As her mind ran with those thoughts, he would also outlive their daughter, Blanche. Now a big smile appeared, how lucky Blanche will be to have him around her whole life.

The smile turned to sadness when she realized how lonely he will become. He had defined the greatest love; she thought I can name the saddest form. When everyone you love is gone and only memories left to cling upon.

He already had many as he called them, carrying them with him, soon Lilith and Blanche will add to that group.

Most of his time was spent writing, currently working on his love story book. She asked him if she was in it? His face turned into a huge smile and his response was, you are the book, with of course you are in it.

She could hear them outside, waiting by the hover craft, they were going to an outdoor show, a play. Blanche was so excited about going, she never was told who her father really was. Barnabas's wishes, he now had a gray beard and mustache but other than that truly little changed about him.

When they found out Bolt had died, she could tell it affected him, he tried to act like it was nothing, but his body deceived his words. He had become a spokesperson for the Core, giving recorded speeches about the benefits of working together, and paid quite well for it.

So many changes had occurred. Then she thought about the future, and how her little monkey would be all alone. That making her feel sad, she was brought out of her thoughts with more yelling from below. Now both Blanche and Barnabas were yelling for her to get going.

Blanche was already siting in the driver's seat, usually Lilith would ride in the front and Barnabas alone in the back. As she saw him, a wave of emotions overwhelmed her, rushing into his arms and kissing him passionately on the lips.

Blanche just watching with a look of disbelief and said, "Really?"

Lilith looking at her beautiful daughter then husband who had given her a life she could not have imagined replied, "Yes." She said it sweetly and then got into the back of the craft with her husband, Barnabas.

Novels by Brad Shprintz

Covers created by Brittany Wilson

www.ingramcontent.com/pod-product-compliance
Lightning Source LLC
Chambersburg PA
CBHW040531170726
48295CB00012B/422